BEWILDERED

BEWILDERED

s t o r i e s

CARLA PANCIERA

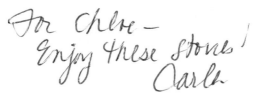

For Chloe —
Enjoy these stories!
Carla

UNIVERSITY OF MASSACHUSETTS PRESS
Amherst and Boston

This book is the winner of the 2013 Grace Paley Prize in Short Fiction. The Association of Writers & Writing Programs, which sponsors the award, is a national nonprofit organization dedicated to serving American letters, writers, and programs of writing. Its headquarters are at George Mason University, Fairfax, Virginia, and its website is www.awpwriter.org.

ISBN 978-1-62534-133-4
Designed by Sally Nichols
Set in ArnhemFine and Avenir
Printed and bound by Sheridan Books, Inc.

Library of Congress Cataloging-in-Publication Data

Panciera, Carla.
[Short stories. Selections]
Bewildered : stories / by Carla Panciera.
pages ; cm
"This book is the winner of the 2013 Grace Paley Prize
in Short Fiction"—Title page verso.
ISBN 978-1-62534-133-4 (jacketed hardbound : alk. paper)
I. Panciera, Carla. All of a sudden. II. Title.
PS3616.A365A6 2014
813'.6—dc23
2014019834

British Library Cataloguing-in-Publication Data
A catalogue record for this book is available from the British Library.

The Grace Paley Prize in Short Fiction is made possible
by the generous support of Amazon.com.

For Beatrice, Apphia, and Justina

CONTENTS

BEWILDERED

ALL OF A SUDDEN

Albinna wore a faded yellow jumper for the fifth grade photo, white socks pulled to her knees. She set her white hand on the top of the fencepost prop and grinned.

Back in the classroom, she stood behind me to sharpen her pencil, eraser worn to a flat, muddy moon. Chips of yellow flickered in her eyes the way sand sparkling in riverbeds makes you think: *gold*. Freckled nose, forehead, tops of hands now that I'd seen them up close.

"Isn't it great they gave us a free comb?" she said.

She didn't need my response.

She could walk to my house, she told me, through the woods. She'd seen the silos. Her teeth were so small, I wondered if any had fallen out yet.

I had a lot of friends, got dropped off at houses that overlooked the ocean or at the homes of artists' children, high-ceiling places where an entire wall might be taken up with a sculpture of angelfish. The builder's daughter had a fireplace in her bedroom, a closet we could dance in, except we never danced. Because I lived on a farm, set apart from the rest of our town, I hadn't met anyone who lived close enough to walk over, who might come for an hour after school several days in a row, whose coming would not be monumental.

But Albinna was one of the new kids, sent to our school because hers was overcrowded. Mine was no longer the last bus stop. Instead, when the others had gotten off, Albinna moved to the seat behind me and we rode with the fumes, the lunch box smell of overripe bananas and cold cuts, the bus driver scanning her rearview.

"I guess you could come over," I said.

Albinna walked into my house that first day the way she always entered places, as if everyone had been talking about her, but she wasn't about to be angry. She was close to apologizing for the interruption, her smile a great attempt at smiling—a hopeful smile with more faith than you might imagine she'd have. She flipped her hair back over one shoulder and stuck her head forward as if peering over a threshold.

My mother turned away from the television on the counter; my father paused over his soup bowl.

"Nice to meet you," Albinna said, before anyone had been introduced. She touched my father's shoulder, offered her pale hand to my mother, not as a handshake, just to clasp fingers, the way I'd seen adults say good-bye on their way out of crowded places.

"We're glad you're here," my father said, which he'd never said to anyone before.

My mother kept her hand for a little while.

Later, my mother said, "She's lovely," which I hadn't noticed. Albinna inspired that kind of surprise.

I remember the place she lived: wood floors worn white, beds unadorned but for white sheets, dark blankets folded at the foot, closets full of empty hangers clicking together, her big white shirt when we didn't wear things like that, her shoes and those of her sisters aligned, the corners of the trundle she shared with one of the girls folded neatly as a gift.

"I'm named for a saint," she said. "Not a famous one."

I looked it up.

"It's spelled wrong," I told her.

The Blessed Virgin, the kind you see in cemeteries, kept watch on a table in the front entrance, bowed neck strung with scapulae. Six children and never a stray teaspoon in the sink. The phone off the hook for days because of her mother's headaches, because one of the girls got caught smoking. Figurines everywhere that her mother paid a quarter for at yard sales. Her father cut recesses in walls for them, like a gift shop display, a kitschy museum. On Saturday mornings, before we met to walk downtown—Albinna had no bike to ride— her mother made her dust them. The kitchen table would be filled with women in pink skirts, their hair piled like ice cream, and men in long coats, tails frozen into black fins, everyone ready for the ball, no cracks about their necks, no missing hands despite the bird-bone narrow shape of them.

Albinna wiped porcelain faces with an old sock, setting them back as gently as eggs in the empty house. "My mother wants everyone out," she'd say.

I'd wait on a rock across the street.

I went to parties she was not invited to. She was the new girl; she still printed her name. These were reasons enough for exclusion. Albinna did not feel sorry for herself the way I felt sorry for her. It was as if she had no expectations of her own. Besides, she gave terrible gifts—panda bear key chains, a felt bag of shiny blue stones. So I went and acted like a popular girl. I had a Danskin suit for pool parties. I knew tricks for making people talk in their sleep.

I imagined Albinna trolling the aisles of the dime store, the sleeves on a denim jacket her brother'd outgrown rolled over her wrists. The saleswomen, older than our mothers, sweaters capelike around hunched shoulders, would follow after her expecting her to pocket lip gloss or musk, things she fingered or picked up to smell. There was nothing she thought of stealing. But who else would have known that about her?

I stopped going places without her. I felt a generous love for her and for myself for loving her. When she couldn't go somewhere because she was ironing curtains, she'd been out that day already, she had to get lettuce at the store, I stayed home, my mother asking: "Where's Albinna today?"

We'd found a rusting truck cap in a back field and dragged an old coffee table into it. She brought a candle and once we tried cigarettes. Days without her, I'd sit there myself, bring the dog, find something to use as a vase and fill it with wild chamomile.

"You could ask another friend over," my mother said, but I had no wish to do that.

—— — ——

Albinna used words wrong, words no one else would get wrong, words that made other girls study her to see if she was serious. I stood amongst them, awkward for Albinna who remained unfazed, who tilted her head at their stares and waited to be let in on something.

So when we were alone as we were summer days, we'd walk and she'd say: "Wouldn't it be great to go to the beach somewhere? Stop walking around the streets like vagamonds?"

"Vagabonds," I'd tell her.

She'd shrug, not angry, not embarrassed. "What's the difference?"

I'd feel my own impatience: If only you'd get this right, I'd think.

She'd say, "I'm not perfect."

In the silence and the heat, we'd resume our tread, me toting a stone of regret. Then Albinna would hang her body, thin as fishing line, over the curb and wave at the empty street.

"All of a sudden, gorgeous guys drive by—hey girls, surf's up!" she said.

And our awkwardness ended. All of a sudden. She liked to say that.

She could never be depended upon to sleep over or to go shopping, or to do anything else we did. Her mother found her at birthday parties and banged on the windows to demand her home. You couldn't get your heart set on the drive-in Friday night or the baseball game after school. Even on Saturdays, when her mother and father went dancing, they insisted she stay in, her sisters out, her brother, too, the youngest child, a boy, asleep on sheets Albinna shook out the window each day. She made sure the television cooled down before they came home so they wouldn't know she'd been watching. Her parents slept in the next morning, sending their thin envelope to Mass with Albinna. Many times they asked her about the sermon and called the rectory to make sure she was right. She didn't ask for reasons. She did not fight back.

One afternoon in his garage, her father's best friend—she called him uncle—put his hand on her knee, a sunburned knee, a tender, warm knee. He said things that made her want to cry, but she pretended it was a joke and hurried out past a workbench strewn with tools.

She was fourteen.

She never told anyone what he did. She told me, fingers playing the tabletop like a piano, the old gold cat on the grapevine outside the window studying her like a fish, like something dazzling and vulnerable beneath the light, the pale flesh of her, the way she flipped her thick hair from one peeling shoulder to the next. She laughed through it, trying to make me laugh, as if he too had been kidding, as if everyone understood the fun in it.

"All of a sudden Batman and his little co-host Robin come in for a screwdriver and I'm out of there," she told me.

She hurried through the story so she wouldn't be late for dinner.

"You could live here," I said. "My parents wouldn't mind."

She pasted on a little smile. "Why would I want to do that?" she said.

When her parents urged her to visit her uncle more often, she refused. They kept her home for a week varnishing their bedroom floor, but she wouldn't change her mind.

That winter she found an old purple sweater, mohair, in my attic. "Keep it," I said, when she tried it on.

She wore it our first year in high school, wore it when we didn't wear old things, wore it on days too warm to wear it, wore it on days when she didn't wear her big white shirt with the pink bra beneath it, a made-up pink, a pink that didn't appear anywhere else in the world. The artists' daughters, the builder's daughter, stared at her back and then at each other.

She walked up to their lunch table one day.

"I'd like to sit down," she said, her smile full of those baby teeth. "If I'm not taking someone's seat."

Surprised, they nodded towards an empty chair. I set my tray down next to hers, pulled another seat over. I felt too close to her, but I didn't know where else to sit. I didn't want to leave her there. Albinna ate her cake first, a flake of white frosting clinging to her lip. She glanced around the silent faces peering into brown bags or picking at the hot stew in the trays before them. She beamed as if she were watching children she adored being absorbed in constructing block towers.

"You're in my algebra class," she said to a girl shoving orange peels into her sack.

The bell sounded for the end of lunch.

"All of a sudden, we think of something to talk about and, bam, it's time to go," Albinna said.

In history class, she rolled her eyes at the bald teacher who sat behind his desk and lectured. I took the notes she'd borrow later. She'd been assigned a seat in the back of the room, surrounded by boys. She wasn't afraid to ask them for gum before class. She tapped their books with her pencil on her way down the aisle. By this time, she was so lovely, long-legged, even I noticed, but she was without crushes or infatuation, was without the obvious need for any of these people.

She mumbled into the pages of her notebook where she practiced her signature: "All of a sudden Jefferson comes in with an extra wig, says, hey mister, wear this. And while you're at it, quit infridgement on their pursuit of happiness."

The boys chuckled. The girls looked her way wondering what the amusement could be.

She sanded her corner shelf in woodshop alongside the tech boys. She painted a mural in art class with girls with purple lips and fishnet stockings. She copied grammar worksheets from the soccer goalie. While I made my way through the halls holding up a quiet hand to those I'd known most of my life, Albinna called out to strangers in every corridor. And they called back.

Invitations came for her to semi-formals and parties over bonfires on the beach. People in the bleachers at basketball games made room for her, boys gathered around her locker where her books sat neatly covered on the shelf. "Come, too," she would say when she told me of her plans, and why didn't I? Why didn't I before she stopped asking? I had forgotten how to act like them, how to talk to them, had made Albinna my friend and had forgotten how to make others.

But mostly, I wanted her to myself. Had assumed I would always have that.

When she stopped coming to my house as often, I begged my mother to teach us to drive standard in the parking lot at Almacs grocery store. I invited Albinna to a restaurant where we could have our tea leaves read. I suggested we try camping.

Albinna chose the tea leaves. It was my sixteenth birthday. My father put on aftershave, my mother counted out money before we left and filed bills into his wallet. Cold rain glossed the dark road out behind the Narragansett Long House. Albinna chattered about palm readers and horoscopes, things her mother warned her about. She told us how she paid a quarter for a tiny scroll that revealed she had a guardian angel, that her lucky color was white. My mother smiled over her shoulder from the front seat, my father glanced at her in the rearview. Albinna had left things behind to be with us.

"I told my mother we were out for Chinese," she said.

"You lied?"

"She doesn't need to know everything about me." Albinna's breath steamed the window she faced. "No one does."

We dumped our tea into water goblets, turned the cups over onto our saucers and spun them three times. Princess Goldwing had a long, gray braid that hung over the chair back. She wore pink framed glasses like a young girl and not deerskin, but a blue tunic with a turquoise clasp at her throat. "You are loyal; you have a stubborn streak," she told me.

But to Albinna she said: "You have the wind for you—see the leaves scattered here, just before the saucer rim? And just as these leaves part, here where there is this path for you: this is love, a very wide path. Follow this and then, there will be no more fear."

That spring, I walked out to meet her by my side of the brook, just before the pine grove. We hadn't met there since my birthday months before, but she had agreed to this day, and I imagined what she'd say, how she would reaffirm our friendship and how relief would surge through us, but of course I wouldn't have it right. This was part of her gift: that she would say what you could never have imagined. Still, I must have had some idea she would stand before me, that year when she was willing to save herself at last, a beautiful girl, a girl with friends. This is how I remember it: her twisting a blade of grass, long hair sliding over her shoulders.

That day I said, "My mother made dinner."

But I already understood how helpless I was.

"Your mother," she said. Then she said she couldn't come. She wouldn't come anymore.

I didn't know then that we were at that age when we make decisions like that, when we don't consider how we might stay together, when we don't understand the value of that kind of work.

I did not say, choose me the way I chose you that day, grinding our pencils to smoke in that classroom. I did not say all the things I've since learned to say, all the things I've practiced.

"You are trying to save me," she said. "Like something in a collection, like the only thing in a collection. You want to be a commiseur of me."

"Connoisseur?" I said.

"And you make me feel bad when you correct me. As if I can't be perfect like you. But you aren't perfect, either."

"I'm not," I said. "I don't feel perfect at all." But she was already going.

It was a long walk home, climbing under the fence, crossing the nut tree field toward the farm laid out before me—the big blue silo at the bottom of the hill, the cow barn where my father must be shaking out hay for the milkers, the calf barn where there was always a baby calling after its mother, and the hayloft where Albinna and I had once found a place carved out by runaways, cans of corn and peas, a rusty jackknife. We had sat a while imagining what it would be like to hide ourselves in that dark, hot place, to be discovered or not, all of sudden, all of a sudden.

The paint peeled off our big white house, a house perched on a ledge, as if washed ashore where there was only one thing to stop it from washing away all together, out of memory. My mother looked over my shoulder when I came in. The doorway behind me framed a setting sun. My mother set three places for dinner.

New things began that day, although not the way I had hoped they would. It wasn't the start of a renewed friendship, of a reclamation. It was, instead, the start of a life where I would be alone for a few years, and where, eventually, I would make new friends, many of them, friends I willed myself to trust. When they looked at pictures of me as a child, I stood apart, and I did not reply when they pointed to my image and said, "I wish I had known you then."

NO SOONER

Robbers, Rita calls them. A word I haven't thought about in years.

She thinks I'm serious when I say: "Like cat burglars." Sleek men dressed in black creeping along apartment building ledges after secret formulas. Marble-jawed martial artists wearing eye masks. It's hard not to think of their haunches, those muscles poised for pouncing.

Oh, but Rita.

She's still chewing the ends of her knitting needles contemplating robbers who, it seems to me, would be fatter and would forgo Spandex for cotton sweatsuits. They'd be more likely to paint their faces with charcoal and screw up the job.

What concerns Rita, truly, are break-ins. The kind that have been happening in this neighborhood. Crimes committed in broad daylight while people are at work. Instead of secret formulas and diamond necklaces, your iPods, your laptops, your accumulation of portable technology go missing.

Rita is my mother-in-law and her son, Michael, and I live in a home that would disappoint even the least acquisitive thief. No necklaces save ones made with macaroni that our twin daughters craft in preschool, little technology except for an Apple IIe computer in our attic and a small color television with rabbit ears on a TV tray in the unheated sun porch. If they're very, very lucky, they might find whole wheat ginger snaps in the pantry and of course, Michael's homebrew in the old Frigidaire, the jugs filled with liquid dark enough to be mistaken for ice coffee.

Michael has taken a half dozen at-risk boys—future perpetrators of break-ins and assorted other felonies—to the Berkshires on an adventure weekend that will feature a ropes course, winter camping and, on the final night, a talent show which, of all the week's activities, will require the greatest amount of trust in one's fellow perps.

Because my daughters and I will be alone with robbers in the neighborhood, Michael has invited his parents to stay with us.

Just in case, he said.

I explained to him, patiently, as he strummed his guitar and penned a few lyrics (he writes children's songs and has sold a few), that one eighty-year-old father, though spry enough to scale a ladder and clean out our gutters twice a year, and one seventy-six-year-old mother who suffers from anxiety attacks, may not be much defense against marauders.

And anyway, I said. Break-ins occur during the day. When no one is home.

They could happen any one of the days I am off with the girls while Michael is at work just a few miles away.

But Michael insisted and since he rarely insists, and there have been many moments in our marriage where I wished he would insist, strong-arm, bully, instead of beaming at me, instead of contemplating, I agree.

I move to the guest room, to the bed I had as a single woman with the same down comforter that makes Michael sneeze atop it. Rita protests. She won't hear of usurping my bedroom, even tries elbowing me out of her way at the top of the stairs, but this time, *I* insist, in the sugary and not really funny joking voice her other children use: "Sweetie, no. I won't have it. Those old bones need a good night's rest if you're going to keep up with me."

She guffaws and says: "Who are you calling old. I'll club ya!"

I pretend to laugh and close the door, slide into bed, delirious. My own room. My own comforter to which I am not allergic. Meanwhile my husband may be bivouacking on the side of a mountain with a boy who knows how to make a bomb from a can of oven cleaner. A hulking boy twice my tiny husband's weight. In my old room, my in-laws debate whether it is safe to soak dentures in bleach since they have left some necessary tablets at home. The girls sleep, Olivia coughing, Skylar flinging off her covers no matter that the house is cold. The house is always very cold.

I miss no one but the lonely single woman I used to be, the yellow apartment walls pitted with holes from where I tried to hang pictures by eyeballing spots only to discover I'd guessed high every time. The kind of moments my sister envisions for herself now that she is divorcing her husband and losing weight. She married out of high school, to the first man she'd ever slept with. Lived her life, raised her children, worried I would never settle down. *Settle down*, is how she put it, which made me imagine myself on the frontier. A pioneer who, after fording rivers and cannibalizing fellow travelers, finds love. Now I wonder why she worried. Unhappy as she must have been. Unsurprised, excited really, as she is now that her union is over.

But I bought into it. The marriage myth. The what's-wrong-with-me-if-I'm-not story. Loved often and wrongly. Fled sometimes and sometimes was deserted. Had given up, relieved, moved into the apartment with the yellow walls when I met Michael. I sold office supplies out of my trunk. Carted a crate of samples into his school. He offered to carry them for me, and I hesitated, worried he would drop them.

"Patty," he said to the secretary, "after you lie and tell her the principal can't see her today, call me and I'll help her out to her car."

The first days knowing him, I sat at my table eating soup and thought: I could never love a man that small, though he was handsome in a fine-boned, sculptured features way. He played songs for me, his tiny shoes off, lined up against the couch as if a boy had left them there on his way to bed. It was terribly embarrassing. But he made me laugh. He made my sister laugh. Funny, she called him, and wise. A man, she told me, concerned with bigger things. And he is. Which was the first reason I loved him.

My dream comes fast: I lie on grass. Summer. I worry about something, recognize that worm in my belly, but webby clouds fill a blue sky. Beside me, a lean young man stretches himself. Latino, with the stubble from such a few facial hairs, I know it is not possible—at least not yet—for him to grow a beard. This youngster. This not-so-handsome boy-man. I recognize as well that feeling that supplants the worry in my stomach. It's farther south and hotter.

I could lie here forever, but he insists on giving me a ring. I dread his gift. I remember the gifts from young men, the ideas they had of what women might love: cloying perfumes and miniscule diamond earring studs. Michael's first gift to me was a packet of giant pumpkin seeds. Then a wheelbarrow full of manure to get them off to a good start. Making my evenly spaced hills, I understood how to begin measuring out the attainable. Oh right, I remember thinking, true love will not blow me away like a powder. True love is the slowest love I will be in.

I believed it would burn so slowly, it would make fire for the rest of our lives together.

The Latino boy puts this ring on my finger, and I make little sounds over it. It fits my pinky. It is metallic red like bike paint. He confesses he had help picking it out. It comes to me, too, that sex, lots of it and quickly done, helps allay relationship doubts. So I kiss him and he kisses back and we are in someone's house, the shades drawn and there are people there. My sister's fattest friend who has also lost weight, but who has dark circles under her eyes, asks if this means we are engaged.

"Oh, that," I say, wishing she would leave.

He will be very patient and will tease me, a neck-kisser, a soft-toucher, and to enjoy this, I will need to banish any thoughts of how to leave him eventually.

I wake to Olivia's coughing, 5 a.m., prop her up on an extra pillow. Outside, the street light illumines an empty street devoid of robbers, but the wind gusts, upends a dried out pot of mums on our front steps, slaps the shrink-wrap on a neighbor's boat. In the kitchen, I brew a small pot of coffee, not the decaf Rita favors. Let me drink every drop and tremble through my morning, empty as it will be of young lovers.

When dawn arrives, it reveals a blue tarp suspended in the bare branches of a tree. This big, winglike, kite-of-a-thing appearing out of the night *is* a gift, its shape slowly realized by light and then all day the question: How did that happen? Where did that come from?

Until Louis wakes and goes outside without breakfast to see what it'll take to get it down and Rita stands at the window muttering: "I wonder would a mop do it?"

She makes herself a cup of instant decaf, toasts the white bread she brought with her and sits down with the paper. She reads it with glasses bought at the drugstore. Same place she buys the boxes of chocolates she gives me every birthday. Mostly, I have simple tastes, but I can't abide cheap chocolate. I thank her, of course, and later Michael and I have a laugh while he follows the map inside the cover to discover all the caramels. He can't resist them, a rare weakness.

"She likes you enough to fatten you up," he says.

"Like Hansel," I say. Though at times I am embarrassed that my husband writes children's songs, performs at birthday parties several times a year, I am always certain he'll understand fairy tale references.

He holds out his finger.

"Not nearly fat enough," I say, taking hold of it, insubstantial as the digits of our daughters. I use it to puncture chocolate after chocolate.

"My father used to buy her the heart-shaped boxes for Valentine's," he said. "The fancier, the better. She was the envy of all her sisters. Imagine that, to have married a thoughtful man. But then she worried about diabetes so she made him stop."

She is lucky that way. My father-in-law adores her. Turns off his animal shows if a snake appears. He walled up the bathroom window so that, during thunderstorms, she'd have a dark retreat to wait out the disturbance, sitting on the tub edge humming to herself. He reads the extended forecast to see if conditions exist for any such weather before they makes plans to leave home and her personal bomb shelter.

Things Michael would probably do for me if I was crazy, but I'm so sane I am comfortable knowing his mother doesn't like me much. Her initial relief that her son wasn't gay or so much of a bohemian that he'd refuse marriage altogether, ebbed once she learned we'd marry on a hillside in Vermont, Michael's old college roommate, a Buddhist monk, presiding. But married is married so she went along, though she wore a blue chiffon dress and pumps that sank into the ground at a reception filled with homebrew and barefoot people who could play guitar.

"I give you a lot of credit," she said to me that day. "Putting up with these people."

True, there weren't many of my friends there, a few people from work and my sister who over-celebrated anything out of the norm. She'd dance and sing and let her kids get filthy all the while collecting stories she'd share with bookclub friends when she returned to earth.

But Michael's friends had embraced me, had walked into Michael's apartment the first time we met and bear-hugged me. Had sat with me in the kitchen as I stirred Michael's stew and asked me questions about myself. About office supplies. A job they found ironic since I myself had no office. I didn't dress like them, couldn't play an instrument or hold a tune. I had never chained myself to a fence to protest a nuclear power plant's presence. But I couldn't explain this to Rita, how they had acted as ushers coaxing me into Michael's world. How I had followed them.

Maybe when we bought this house in a real neighborhood, affordable, within walking distance to a school but purely by accident, Rita's hope that her oldest son would be just like his two brothers returned, but the doula-assisted home birth ended that.

"Why do you let him talk you into these things?" she asked. "God, he's foolish."

"He makes sense to me," I told her. To lots of people. He still does. Maybe this is the first reason I love him. The first reason I'd never leave him, though, is it might convince his mother she's right.

I offer to make Rita a pot of decaf.

"God, no," she says. "Louis will go out and get me a cup if I want it."

The girls come downstairs, Olivia in her favorite dress, heavy cotton with red dogs on it, purple tights, Skylar in her shortie pajamas, her pale legs cool as marble. She'll insist I pick something out for her, lay immobile while I dress her. Olivia will cry hot tears Wednesday or Thursday for Michael. Skylar will study her and then curl up on my lap, suck her thumb.

"No mention of any robberies yesterday," Rita tells me. She makes note of the walkers who pass, the fat man and his fat dog, the women whose voices travel through their scarves, through our storm windows.

I set toast down in front of the girls who jabber at one another. Skylar pulls at my shirt, keeps me against her for a minute before letting go.

"Everyone's out and about early," Rita says. "That fellow's already been by twice. I wonder how far does he go?"

The twins shake cinnamon onto their toast. It lands in one lump on the center of the bread.

"You let them eat like this?" Rita says. "I would no sooner give my kids that much sugar . . ." (This part of the sentence she always leaves off).

"Michael doesn't like it, either," I say. "We're celebrating girl week."

We've also planned to paint our toenails and take bubble baths. Things Michael wishes we wouldn't do. Things we most likely won't do with Rita and Louis present. So I've made promises I can't keep. It's how it goes with girls, the beginning of a much more complicated mythology. It starts with little lies and the little disappointments they spawn. Tilled soil for mid-life erotic fantasies.

My father-in-law pounds away in my basement, putting up pegboards for the tools we may someday own. He's organized paint cans, sucked up cobwebs with a vacuum he brought. Daily, he examines the lint filter in the dryer to be sure I haven't forgotten to clean it out. Rita has read that kind of negligence burns houses down.

Rita calls down the stairs: "Why don't you take a break. I'll make you a cup of coffee."

No answer.

She shakes her head. "He'll kill himself with all the chores around here."

"Why, we've no more use for a pegboard than we have for trained elephants," I say.

Rita stares at me. Blinks.

"We have no tools," I explain.

"Listen, you can't live like this forever." She dunks her own tea bag in and out, in and out of her cup. Decaf. No sugar.

They would like to think this. That their hippie son with his unimaginably small hands would one day saw things down. What must his father have thought when this son didn't grow? Two others did.

But not Michael, the oldest. Oh, Michael got a beard, his voice deepened. His voice is so deep he adds great bass refrains that crack the twins up. But his father, a handyman, a man drawn to post-game analysis, a man whose first job had been hauling granite slabs out of quarries, is two of him. His brothers split wood on weekends, drive enormous pickup trucks to work in the financial district. His bull-shouldered mother, an expert spring cleaner, shoves refrigerators and armoires out of her way seeking dust.

Can you live any way forever? I want to ask Michael, not his mother who stares out at the neighbor across the street checking his box for yesterday's mail. Michael has answers for a question like that, answers that make me stop fretting and fall asleep.

I drop the girls off at Friends of the World Preschool where Miss Sarah has a crush on my husband who plays for them several times a year.

"So how's Michael?" she asks. "Have you heard from him?"

She wears boiled wool socks, new Birkenstocks. A mountainous woman with hair so short, her neck is shaved. I mistook her for an ex-nun, but Michael informed me she's Jewish. Studying for a master's degree with a thesis on teaching children to sing on key. She calls Michael, star of her bibliography, from the library several times a week.

"To have me consider various theories," Michael says, a bowl of raw pea pods on his lap. He stops eating long enough for their conversation then resumes as he fills me in. "What would happen, for example, if you got a child to hold the wrong note while you sang the right one? Like a human tuner, see? Would they catch on? I think they would."

"Is that your final answer?" I say, myself not a woman of theories.

I tell Miss Sarah that Michael cannot reach us. That if we do hear from him, it will not be good news. I laugh, but she looks stricken. The room smells of gingerbread another teacher is baking. My daughters dash off, their coats still on, towards a large table with bowls of raisins and tubes of frosting.

Then I feel bad for Miss Sarah, an enormous virgin who appreciates my husband. I think of the Latino boy's face in my shoulder and a thrill runs through me.

"Really, Michael will be fine. He loves these kids."

"Well, someone ought to," Miss Sarah says. "Leave it to him."

———

While I am prying myself away from Miss Sarah and her cozy morning, three houses down from me several pieces of computer equipment, a digital camera, a telescope, are removed from a house with a Great Dane at home.

"I wonder was it that green van?" Rita says when Louis comes in to tell us. He's been shearing our hedges with clippers I've never seen. Receives the news from a dog walker.

"You saw something?" I say.

"Well it passed a couple times, an old rustbucket and I thought: now who the hell would drive around in that thing?"

When a police officer, moving door to door in search of possible witnesses, arrives to question us, Rita jams her fist in her mouth and stares at the linoleum.

"Do you remember seeing any vehicles along the street this morning?" the officer says.

Rita rocks back and forth.

"No, no," she says to my floor. "How about you, Dad?"

"What's that?" Louis says, thirty inches from the man's badge.

When the officer leaves I ask why they didn't tell him the truth.

"Oh, God," Rita says. "We don't want our names in the paper."

Then she hurries off to the bathroom.

"Well," Louis says. "I'll be on the porch sanding windowsills."

Then he calls in the direction of the closed bathroom door: "I'll have a cup of coffee, Mother, when you get 'round to it."

"Mother of Christ, Dad, you'd think your legs were broken," she hollers back.

Mother. Dad. I've asked Michael does he think they call those names out to each other in their lovemaking.

He says: Only as foreplay as in, *Well, Mother, what do you think?* And, *Mother of Christ, Dad, what's gotten into you all of a sudden?*

That night, Louis climbs the stair with a two-by-four and slides it under the bed.

"What in the name of Jesus are you going to do with that?" Rita asks him.

"We ought to have something up here just in case," he says.

This night's dream I stand on a second floor landing of an apartment building and peer down into the entryway where someone bangs on a locked door. Reverberating pounding in a movie-set setting. The banisters well oiled, the light from far above, stories away and yellow. Alone, I contemplate the strength of that lock but I don't feel scared exactly, only worried again, that chronic gut spiral.

When someone else shows up, I am grateful more than anything for the company. Although he is a celebrity—a sports anchor, ex-quarterback, Kansas blond—I sense our familiarity. He calls down a good-natured threat and the noise ceases. In my apartment, the cabinets are dark wood, the countertops gold linoleum. The quarterback sits on a wooden chair beneath a phone, also gold, its cord so long you could drag the receiver around the room. We have sex, this bigger than life man, this married man. If he does call me Mother here, I will accept the flattery, that he calls me that although I have nothing to do with his children. It is great sex, the kind that lovers surprise each other with in the beginning. Here is something to keep out of context: this act, its pure pleasure. From this dingy room, we will go forth into marriages with other mates. And no one will discover us, hate us the way they would if they knew what we did to good people.

That morning, when Louis flips to the news, I stroll onto the freezing porch and glance at the screen, but my lover isn't there, and I realize how embarrassed I would be if he was, feeling so plainly the fine, white hairs on his thighs. I tote him around all day like a crush, stop at the library to Google him that afternoon, discover his college sweetheart wife, his daughter blind from birth. Blind. So he couldn't leave his family. And where could we hide, this celebrity and I? I imagine huts in the South Pacific, villas in France, a cell in an abandoned convent on an Italian hillside. Michael with his small hands home playing a new song with the girls' names in it. Skylar the brilliant-physicist-watercolor-artist and Olivia the hand-surgeon-rare-lily-breeder.

My sister calls and whispers: "How's it going?"

"Why are you whispering?" I ask.

"Right," she says, laughing. My sister who has never laughed so abruptly in her life now explodes regularly with mirth. "They can't hear me, can they?"

"No one can hear me, either," I say.

Rita and Louis are off to the drugstore, compelled to search out the mystery tablets for their teeth. The bleach, Rita tells me, makes her sneeze which, in turn, nearly knocks her choppers out as soon as she gets them in.

"Is it terrible?" my sister asks.

"It isn't terrible," I say. I would never tell her about the dreams. "But I have been thinking how much they don't like their son. How every chore Louis does around here galls him. So we have a messy basement. It doesn't make us murderers."

"It's not like you would have affairs or anything," my sister says. Before I can ask her where that comes from, she starts to cry.

"Is Emmit having an affair?" I ask. I picture my brother-in-law in his gray t-shirt, his baseball cap, his robber belly looping over his belt.

Through the sniffling and snuffling, I think I hear a no.

"Anyway, even if he was, it's not really an affair since you're separated, is it?" I say.

Abruptly, the crying stops.

"Not technically, but it makes you feel a little crazy," she says.

"Are *you* having an affair?"

I am angry enough to hang up the phone. Also nauseous. My sister's desires to date have centered around granite countertops (unfulfilled) and a Caribbean cruise (fulfilled last April as a final attempt to save the marriage. Might have worked, too, had Emmit not been seasick and spent the entire time in their cabin while my sister dolled herself up for dinner then cried herself to sleep by nine every night). Now this. As if I have a right to hate her because she might be living one of my dreams. But suddenly I feel like shouting: How could you leave me here like this? Married. Monogamous.

"Just once," she says. "And it was a little awkward. When it was over, I just remembered a lot of rustling and breathing. I felt about a hundred years old. I felt guilty."

"What did you expect?" I ask.

"Nothing," she says. "I had no expectations. Where would I have gotten those?"

"But you're single again," I say. "It must have occurred to you you'd have sex."

"I haven't thought much about it. Between custody arrangements and figuring out how we can afford to leave each other. I thought about not having sex with Emmit anymore. What that would be like."

Oh, sister who lacks imagination, I thought. As if the Latino boy, the gridiron hero, stand waiting outside family court, a mall of men just for fucking when you finally get the chance. Truthfully, Michael is a good lover, a man well aware that his partner would never be distracted by glistening pectorals or the impressive weight of a man who could make her surrender if he so chose. But he is my husband.

"Who?" I ask. Demand, really, bracing myself, hoping: please don't let him be beautiful.

The brother of her fattest friend, the woman from my dream. I can't conjure him. But I pray for fat genes then ask for forgiveness. From what god? From the clock on the wall.

"Well," I ask. "Will you see him again?"

"I think so. I mean, I guess."

Then she laughs again in a burst, gets another call and abruptly ends ours. My sister who no doubt will be out shopping for underwear some time today.

When Rita returns, she waves the pharmacy bag triumphantly.

"Great," I say. "Congratulations. What'd you do with Louis?"

"Oh, Christ, we passed a hardware store and he wants to go back, stock up on some stuff. You know, Daddy tries to do this stuff for the other boys, but they'd no sooner need his help than . . . Anyway, they don't want him dropping dead doing stuff they can damn well do themselves."

Michael would ignore her, or laugh and say: Just think, if he drops dead in our basement, it may be months before anyone ventures down there to find him.

But I say: "We don't want Louis to drop dead, either, believe it or not. Even we are not that horrible."

Rita shouts out one giant laugh. She will turn it into a joke. She will back away from replies. She prefers to lay a statement out and have it reverberate off ceiling tiles, unchallenged by anything but plants and sunlight. I will be the first woman to love her son forever. No matter what. Anything less would be sending him back. I refuse to cry.

"I was just thinking," I say. "Michael will be home tomorrow. There's no need for you and Louis to stay tonight."

"You'll be afraid alone," she says.

My turn to laugh.

"We'd no sooner have a break-in here than you and Louis would join a club for swingers," I say.

"Louis, a dancer? You've got to be joking," she says.

"Go. Really."

Rita picks at her bottom lip. "Oh, but I thought . . . I mean, I just . . . Let me ask Dad."

——

My last dream, back in my own bed on clean sheets, I marry a quiet man, tall with a heart-shaped face. He has two children at the ceremony and one, a small girl, follows us past an in-ground pool, its water green, algae clouds skimming surface. She falls in and he goes after her, me in my wedding dress, simple, Jackie Kennedy-ish, peering into the filmy green depths to witness heroics.

Then, dry, we walk to the church though we are already married and I wonder, What happened to his first wife? Consider Googling her on my honeymoon. Tell myself I watch too much Court TV when I am alone, shivering on the porch, when my real husband, saver of fledglings muscled out of nests, freer of spiders on the bathroom wall, volunteers at a suicide hotline. My best-friend-husband whose childlike hands on my body conjure images for closed-eyed me of Asian women lovers.

My dream husband, his wan complexion, mouse-brown hair, his daughter clinging to the leg of his tux, looks into my face. Suspects things about me that other men could never guess, kinder men, men more deserving of devotion. You will never leave me, his expression says. Threatens. Something my real husband would never say. Anyway, in the dream it is too late. We have these children. I have let them grow fond of me. People have watched us do this, have carried silver gift boxes around the edge of the filthy pool. Celebrating witnesses who believe in unions. Believe our love. The fear that bores into me takes over worry's runnels.

I wake to a noise, sit up in the center of my bed, listen for the shape the noise will take, a doorway silhouette, in the hallway a shushing. A crouching intruder, no comic strip character, but someone who has climbed out of an unsuspecting lover's bed to be here. Who will use insomnia as alibi, who knows all the tricks for taking his woman's mind off her gut.

I think of the 2x4 Louis has no doubt returned to the basement. A weapon I'd swing uselessly anyway. I think of the girls across the hall. Olivia will have her bare legs exposed. Skylar's eyelids, faint purple, will twitch. They sleep as if nothing will ever harm them. Not while I am here.

What am I supposed to say to that? That it's all been carved out for us already? That we're all just as safe as we are happy? I don't have the answers Michael does, the ones that let us fall back to sleep, let us dream. We women who hear noises in the night and know, despite our fantasies, our only chance is that a good man will save us.

BEWILDERED

Meet Ben Oates, former class vice-president (high school and college), who got his homework in on time and never broke curfew. Ben who had no five-year plan, no vision for his future or anyone else's, who checked off assigned tasks as they were completed and ended up in college, law school, partners' meetings. Also ended up marrying the first woman who loved him back. Gorgeous woman who strode into his favorite lunch place on a day when the only place to sit was beside him. Sure, it's felt too easy, when he's had a chance to reflect, when he feels inclined to assess. Mostly, he acknowledges he's lucky and spends his life trying to atone for it.

Meet Ben's coffee table, that pile of lumber beneath the Japanese maple on his front lawn. Here where power lines are buried and starlings ready to loiter between poles look elsewhere for amusement, Ben climbs out of his first BMW and scratches his head. He will have to ask Mirabelle Joy, his stunning wife—he's nicknamed her Bella Bride—what happened. He can hear the 1950s version of himself opening the front door and saying, "Now, what's this all about?" However, in real time, as Ben shuffles to the mudroom entrance where he'll leave his shoes on the mat, he remembers: the night before, he had once again forgotten to use a coaster. He inhales.

Bella, and she is, let's face it, one of the most beautiful women he's ever seen, is bent into the oven checking a pot roast she's secured in a browning bag. Through the steam, he spies the baby carrots he used to be so fond of. Now they have them three or four nights a week. He finds them tucked into his suit pockets and in the glove compartment of his car.

Before he can say (if he ever intended to, which he didn't): What happened to the coffee table? Bella turns, the smell of pot roast and camellia bubble bath on her and says, "If you refuse to take care of our things, they may as well be destroyed. I'm through living with animals. I thought we both agreed: this is our dream house."

Their baby sleeps in his playpen, curtains lifting over him in a breeze. Bella follows Ben upstairs where he intends to change out of his suit. She sits on their bed and contemplates him for a minute and then pulls him to her and kisses him passionately.

"Why do you make me do such naughty things?" she says, baby voice, and then unzips his pants.

———

"Well, she is a bit unstable," Eloise, his mother-in-law, says when he drops off her prescriptions the next day. "But you knew that."

One of the goats is getting her hooves trimmed in the kitchen, Eloise's brown hands with their gigantic knuckles working the blade the way Mirabelle peels carrots, even the baby ones.

"I guess you also knew there's no return policy."

Ben Oates, alumnus of the top all-boys private high school in the country, ski house on a mountain base, cellar of port, nods at his mother-in-law's goat.

The animal nibbles drawer handles and chair backs while Eloise inspects the pills. When the goat noses over, she feeds her the drug interaction sheet.

"What Mirabelle needs," Eloise tells him, "is to be listened to. She can achieve that one of two ways. She can talk about any subject under Mars while people stare at her, or she can throw a tantrum. You've got to appear to be her audience whether you're drowning her out or not."

In Mirabelle's jewelry box is a pin that says *No, I am not a model.* She used to wear it to bars. At his ten year reunion, his high school classmates—he can't call them friends although they'd vote him into office, they'd offer him jobs in their fathers' companies—had attractive wives. But they stared at Mirabelle, her mass of red curls, her big eyes the color of sea-glass. She could talk science and politics, sports and opera. She could make you laugh. She could fuck your brains out in the parking lot. There are many days he can't believe she chose him.

Friday the firm closes early to celebrate their thirtieth anniversary. His colleagues head to Simmy's for drinks. Ben, youngest junior partner in the history of the firm and thus their superior, goes but doesn't say much. The next week, he knows, they won't ask him. This is how it goes for Ben. He'd join a fraternity or play rec baseball, never miss a meeting or a practice,volunteer for fundraising and community outreach, impress people with his dependability. His father congratulated him for being president of this, chairperson of that. His mother said, "That's wonderful dear. Invite your new friends over for dinner."

Once or twice he did, but then they'd get enough money for the new press box or the blood drive was a rousing success, and he would have nothing more to discuss with them, would stand amongst the laughing crowd at campus bars while his beer got warm and wonder what people talk about.

That Mirabelle loves him is miracle enough. That he gets to stay home and move from one of her rooms to the other is the real gift. So leaving Simmy's, at least he has that: not the gift of conversation, but the ability, the marital requirement, to sit quietly and listen.

He leaves the bar so early, it is still light out when he pulls into his driveway. The goat on his front lawn startles him. He thinks: deer, but then it bleats and strips the yellowing leaves off a bleeding heart. He wishes he'd had the second beer. In his bay of the garage, Eloise's van sits with the cargo door open.

"Do you have any idea how much trouble you're in?" he says. The goat ambles towards him, maaa-ing. To look for the raisins she feeds them, Eloise's goats will tear the pockets off people. Ben considers the distance to his house. He's just about to make a run for it when the door opens and Mirabelle howls.

"Filthy, filthy beast!" she screams. It takes Ben a beat to realize she's speaking to the goat.

Eloise appears behind her, the same curls but gray and frizzy. She drums her lips with her fingers.

"Should've brought Basil, instead," she says. "I'd forgotten Lily knows all about door handles."

Once she hears that voice, Lily ignores Ben and follows Eloise into the van. Eloise clicks a leash onto the goat's collar and ties her to the steering wheel.

"You shouldn't bring them anywhere at all, you crazy woman!" Mirabelle says. She will want to inspect the damage but won't chance getting shit on her house shoes. Instead she cranes a swan's neck toward the bleeding heart and a heavily chomped arrangement of sedum and cabbage. "Look at my sedum. Did you consider that replacing it this late would be almost impossible? That a trip to the nursery for leftovers isn't high on my to-do list?"

Eloise secures the van door and swats the air between her and her daughter. "Could be worse," she says. "You could have a rabbit problem. Try ordering them around. Next time you have a fussy baby, call someone with house cats."

Then she climbs into the driver's seat, backs out the driveway and down the road as far as they can see.

Monday, the police call Mirabelle who is having a bath, so she calls Ben.

"If the sign says haddock, oughtn't it be haddock? How should I have known it was cod?"

Ben asks again why she is crying, what the police have to do with the fish and is the baby okay. He's beginning to wonder how the child can sleep so much.

"It's not the fish, Ben. It's Eloise. She's had an accident at the Super Y, which reminds me of my own horrible morning there."

He asks his secretary to reschedule an important meeting—efficient Gayle who spends her lunch hour studying for night school classes, who wears shirts that never need ironing.

"I'll tell them your wife is ill," she says. At first this shocks him because he wonders if Gayle has discovered something, but then he understands it is the perfect excuse. His gratitude surprises him less than the extent of his good fortune. Gayle had started as a temp three years ago. Some random name plucked out of the Needs Placement file at an employment firm he couldn't have named even if he was tortured for the information.

The supermarket parking area is, as they will say in the six o'clock news, cordoned off, but he is family (family?!). Where there used to be a window decorated with Halloween coloring contest pictures, a hole gapes, chunks and splinters of glass glittering in a cold, bright sun.

Eloise sits stone-faced on the handi-scooter, police officer crouched beside her taking notes. Between check-outs seven and twelve sits the accordioned version of Eloise's blue van, its windshield covered with brown bags, cereal boxes, a birthday cake.

When Ben approaches her, she looks up and whimpers: "Don't hurt me."

The officer stands and places a hand on Ben's shoulder.

"She didn't take her medication," Ben explains, red-faced.

Store clerks huddle in the express line. The manager is someone Ben went to grammar school with, someone without Ben's breaks. Nice kid who got chosen in the middle of the pack for kickball and who never brought egg salad for lunch. Ben's embarrassment is not about his mother-in-law who might have assumed the grocery store had a drive-thru, but for his own good suit, thick head of hair.

He brings Eloise home. She's worried the goats will be hungry and disturb the neighbors. Mirabelle doesn't answer the phone the first several times he calls her.

"Someone has to clean the top of the refrigerator," she snaps when she finally answers. "I'm sure that never occurs to you."

Eloise stares out at people raking leaves and opening mailboxes.

"Was the child hurt?" she says to the window.

"There was no child, Eloise. You confused the gas for the brake."

He has his crazy wife who dazzles people, a pleasant kid who sleeps through the night and otherwise makes himself unnoticeable, and up until this afternoon, an eccentric mother-in-law who at least understood the burden of her daughter. Now, he feels adrift, as airborne as Eloise must have been moments before settling into the Super Y checkouts.

He could go to his own parents and say what? Mom, Dad, I've married a woman who has smashed a coffee table when I didn't use a coaster, who has tossed my dirty clothes on the front lawn because I didn't put them in the hamper before I showered, who has poured Windex over a perfectly fine lasagna because I said, "You usually make a red sauce"?

His mother, in a nylon track suit deadheading geraniums in window boxes, his father building model airplanes on a workbench in the garage, would clear their throats in unison and say, "Marriage is full of ups and downs, isn't it, dear?"

It took two years after his retirement for his father to stop smelling of gasoline and grease. He promised his wife new carpet as soon as he sold the garage, though she had never complained. They are proud of their only child—a little overwhelmed by his wife, by his big house and his vacations. They sit at his table and keep their hands folded on their laps until Mirabelle starts eating. They ask before they use the bathroom.

When Ben pulls into his driveway, he hears a noise that sounds like tweeting, but it's the flying goose weathervane turning northeast. The baby sleeps belly down on his playmat in front of the fireplace. So he does play, then wears himself out. Bella is on the phone leaving the same message over and over for friends she rarely speaks to anymore: "I really need to talk to someone. Call as soon as you get this."

He reaches into the refrigerator for a bottle of water and while she talks, he pretends he has a therapist to whom he says: My wife is going crazy.

His therapist, a woman with her hair cut short as a man's, with glass beads over a loose fitting, heavy cotton dress, says: So she was sane before you married her?

He hesitates, then grins and admits: Well, there was that time we rented the sailboat with some other couples for the Jazz Fest.

Friends of yours? Even the pretend therapist seems surprised.

It was expensive. We needed a crowd. Anyway, we brought smoked bluefish and sheep cheese. But it rained, poured. I thought it'd be romantic to sit on deck and tough it out, to watch her salty clothes cling to her, but she sulked and said, "If it's getting wet you want," and dove overboard. Had to be rescued by the Coast Guard. I told them we were horsing around and she went over.

That all?

He nods. She waits. She has several clocks that keep time without numbers, whose pendulums swing silently as if dipping into syrup.

I don't know if you count this, but once when I was absorbed in this really great book, she cut a good-sized chunk of hair out of the back of my head.

The pretend therapist wants to know how these things make him feel.

It takes him a while to come up with: Bewildered.

Mirabelle hangs up the phone and turns to him. "Jason Winsheek wants to build a house next door. The cop?"

Ben doesn't know him.

"His family moved into his grandfather's house next door to us after their dad was killed in Vietnam."

With what is Bella Bride annoyed: With history? With this man's misfortune? With Ben? Then she softens and he is struck by his love for her. An old feeling. Light travels beneath her skin, a reminder of the first mornings he awoke beside her and she snuggled against him. It might have been her day to drive senior citizens to their gardening club or to deliver bagels to a neighbor whose sister had died. She wouldn't be late because she needed so little time to get ready. They'd make sleepy love and then she'd soap his back in the shower and go out without drying her hair or putting on makeup.

"Nice kid and all," she says, and the face changes again, the disturbed Bella back. "But he'll have guns. There'll be people with scores to settle knocking on his door at all hours."

Maybe you should suggest she talk to someone, his therapist says. He's surprised she's still listening but remembers that's her job. He also remembers Eloise's advice so he watches his wife and tries to look sympathetic—though for the first time he wishes Eloise hadn't been as indulgent with Mirabelle as she is with her goats.

"You sound concerned," he says.

She stares at him and bursts into bitter laughter. "Are you the voice at the other end of the consumer complaint line? It's time you got *concerned*, sweetheart, for the safety of your family, for the resale value of your home. It might *concern* you to know he plans on doing the finish work himself. Bet you didn't think that, when we plunked down all the money for this place, we'd end up living next door to some do-it-yourselfer."

What does a man of action, a moderately good looking, financially secure individual, Mr. Mainstream Lucky Boy himself, do in a situation like this? Not *this* as in this conversation, not *this* as in the day he's had rescuing his mother-in-law, but *this* as in this marriage? He picks up the (finally) crying baby, studies a face much more like his fleshy one than like his wife's luminous, sharp-angled one. The baby tenses in Ben's arms.

"He's hungry," Ben says, but the door slams and a car starts. Mirabelle drives away and takes her breasts with her.

The baby cries until he vomits all over his father.

—— • ——

During their first year in this house, whenever Mirabelle went out, Ben studied the earrings in her jewelry box or smelled the sleeves of her blouses. Then he brought a snack into the living room, turned up the volume on the basketball game and opened a beer, all the while listening for the garage door so he could right things before she walked in. He had loved her walking in. Was that possible? Had he looked forward to the reunion rather than steeling himself for the outburst?

Lately, he wondered what to do with her. He was tired of bracing himself, of anticipating reactions that grew less and less predictable. She wasn't perfect herself. News flash. She had no idea how to make a good pot of coffee. Tofu gave her gas. But he'd allowed her to make the rules. For once, he'd let someone else take charge. So this is how it feels, he remembers thinking, a life where someone else takes charge. What had he expected?

When Mirabelle doesn't return after an hour, he calls his mother who asks no questions. The baby cries until his grandmother walks in, coos at him like a pigeon and hustles him upstairs. Ben spreads the newspaper over the kitchen table and eats salsa on Ritz crackers. He hasn't read this much of the paper in months. He makes it to the classifieds before his mother comes down.

"He's whimpering in his sleep, poor love," she says, spitty cloth on her shoulder. "Wouldn't touch this." She dumps a bottle of milk down the sink.

He thinks of asking her to stay. Begging her, really. It's not being alone with his son. That part, he's surprised to think, is comforting now that he's quiet. But Ben has a dim memory of coming off the school bus, of holding back tears and of his mother waiting inside and gathering him up as he flung open the door and sobbed.

"If he wakes up during the night, try applesauce. Of course, Mirabelle will be home by then."

Then he does sob. His mother freezes in the doorway. After a few minutes, he shakes his head.

"Everybody fights, Benjamin. Why, your father and I haven't agreed on which news anchor is best in forty-three years. We couldn't believe our luck when remotes were invented and I could watch Dan Rather during Tom Brokaw's commercials."

She pats his shoulder on her way out.

He had just finished a shower when his mother arrived, the baby wailing in his crib, and now he stands on his porch in his bathrobe waving her off. Bella's chrysanthemums bloom russet and gold, her burning bushes flame, her shiny gourds are perfectly arranged in a basket on the seat of a rocking chair no one dares sit in.

The baby sleeps all night and eats the applesauce his grandmother suggested in the morning. He sucks an ounce of formula from a bottle then amuses himself with the nipple while Ben phones Gayle. She'll re-schedule everything, his absence as seamless as the thin sheet of ice he discovered in the useless bird bath this morning when he'd scanned the driveway for Mirabelle's car.

He calls Eloise though he knows Mirabelle wouldn't have gone home. He doesn't say she's missing, but he does tell Eloise about the new neighbors.

"That'll be the younger son," Eloise says. She'll be standing at her counter, pouring warm goat's milk through a sieve. "Boy bailed his drunken brother out of more messes. Ended up selling the grandfather's place soon as he died so he could get the brother into rehab. I think it worked, too, but it took some doing. Those boys waited for the school bus with Mirabelle and never had warm clothes. Mirabelle drove me crazy bringing hot chocolate out to them, pretending she was always so late, she had to drink it at the bus stop. Spent a week's salary on Styrofoam cups every winter."

Ben discovers clothes for his son. He wonders what they do all day, his crazy wife, his complacent child, and decides to go for a walk. It's a new development with room for up to forty houses, but there are only six or seven now, giant things with natural shingles, decks on three levels, au pair suites over garages. He'd felt so fortunate finding this spot, being able to choose among so many lots. Mirabelle impressed him with her knowledge of architectural drawings and construction materials, but before the framing stage was over, he'd called her a know-it-all. Under his breath, of course, and while standing next to a shrieking power saw.

The baby sleeps almost immediately. No one's out to wave. No cars pass. He hears birds in the underbrush at the roadside, but they refuse to show themselves and he can't blame them, what with all the missed opportunities they have for perching.

The police car startles him as it turns the corner. So this is how one gets news, out wandering on a frosty morning through one's empty, exclusive neighborhood.

Tell me what you felt seeing that car, his therapist might ask him later.

Apprehensive. He'll try to remember that word.

Because you thought she was dead?

His trademark pause, but this time, he's really trying to figure something out.

Because I had time to think about a reaction and I didn't know how people react to such things.

They react the way they react. With grief, with shock, with horror.

He knows therapists go to school for this stuff. They play act and role reverse and all those things that made him terribly uncomfortable when he'd stumbled into a beginning psychology course in college. But *they react the way they react*? What kind of a response is that?

The window slides down and Jason Winsheek introduces himself. Not news of Bella, but the opportunity to meet the new neighbor. Ben is silenced for a moment and then, though he hopes his therapist has retreated by now, bitterly disappointed.

What kind of a monster, his therapist might say, is crushed when the news isn't bad? If therapists say such things, if there are times when they can't help but judge someone. Ben would have no answer no matter how long he sat there on her imaginary couch and temporized.

"Hey, neighbor," Jason says, extending his hand.

Ben doesn't want to appear unjolly. He's never been accused of snobbery. He received his earliest accolade winning a Brotherhood poster contest in third grade. But his handshake is damp, he struggles to say hello, shifts nervously from foot to foot as Jason gets out of his car.

Jason surveys Lot 17 and says, "Feel like I'm coming up in the world."

Suddenly, Ben is so happy for this man, he feels tears again and looks away. Here finally is someone whose fortunes are changing. Who's earned it. Who can look behind him and see a trail of hard work, goal setting. Ben imagines Jason Winsheek sitting on his deck, taking the beer Ben offers him.

"You've got a beautiful place," Jason says. "We don't want anything that fancy. Promised the wife a porch, but she's not particular. Says she wants the house to say 'Welcome.' Crazy woman." But he's chuckling. "Speaking of women, Mirabelle Joy is one of the nicest people I'll ever know. You're a lucky man."

The baby wakes up, looks at Jason and wails. Ben says he needs lunch and hurries up his driveway without saying a proper good-bye, the carriage rocking with the protests of his son. Ben's panic rises as the screams increase, but when he lifts him from the carriage, the baby nestles into his shoulder and relaxes with a few sniffles. Jason waves in one big arc and drives away.

While the baby naps, Ben tries to burn the coffee table lumber he'd piled in the back yard. He likes the idea of sitting here while the sun recedes and watching something burn, but the wood won't catch and he's afraid the baby will wake up so he heads back to his empty house.

On the third day of Mirabelle's absence, worry creeps in. He calls the friends she called her last night home. No one has heard from her since her message. None returned her calls.

"We're all so busy with babies these days," one of them says.

Another asks how long she's been missing. "What do the police say?" she asks.

Ben says he hasn't spoken to the police.

The woman asks what he's waiting for.

It's not Jason Winsheek at his door. It's the uniformed officer who sat with Eloise at the Super Y. There's also a stoop-shouldered, balding detective in a brown leather jacket with a sheepskin collar who asks questions, his eyes taking in the details of Bella Bride's home. Ben allows the uniformed officer to look around.

"Drove off Thursday night," the detective mumbles, taking notes on what Ben says. "Why was she so angry?"

Ben starts to answer, then stops. Instead, he says, "She's been off-balance lately."

The detective frowns, taps his pen against his clipboard. He doesn't ask for elaboration, just waits until Ben continues: "Like the other night when I didn't use a coaster? She blew it out of proportion."

"Kind of frustrating, is it? I mean, you work hard and have to come home to this stuff? Wipe your feet, put the seat down." He shakes his head and snorts.

Ben feels the relief he'd anticipated feeling hanging out with Jason Winsheek.

Someone understands, he tells his therapist and gets no reply which he takes for agreement.

"It really is," he says to the detective. "She's making *me* crazy."

The detective's smile disappears just as the back door opens and the cop says, "There's something you ought to see."

The baby fusses in Ben's arms as the men stand over a pile of wood that used to be a coffee table.

———

All of the following facts are true: he and his wife had disagreements; he entertained fantasies of a life without her; he did, at times, feel uncommonly devoted to her; he had spoken to a police officer on the morning after her disappearance and had not voiced his concerns for her whereabouts; he had showered before his mother arrived and had thrown the clothes he had worn during his last argument with Mirabelle immediately into the washing machine; he had sobbed in his mother's presence; his mother-in-law had been afraid of him that day in the supermarket; he had tried to destroy the smashed furniture. Also true that he had lied to the Coast Guard about how Bella fell overboard, and that his wife was generous, warm, intelligent, gorgeous, well-loved, a devoted mother. And that she is missing.

Well, Ben is a lawyer, for a little while longer anyway. He doesn't need a detective in a cheap imitation of a fighter pilot's jacket to spell it out for him. He spends hours with the police. They don't drink coffee and smoke cigarettes during the interrogation. They do wait for Ben's colleague to arrive before questioning him. Still, they don't hide their contempt, their assurance of his guilt, their hunger for him. That first day, he believes they'll figure out who he is, not a celebrity and not a murderer, just a do-gooder, another example of the seriously improbable suspect. People will speak on his behalf (but they won't), the detectives will unearth the records of his charitable contributions (but they don't), Mirabelle will return and explain everything (but she never does). Still, they have to let him go.

His father has a heart attack and when Ben enters the hospital ward, his mother says, not unkindly, "It will upset him to see you." When Gayle asks for a reference she closes the office door, presses her back against it and says, "I'm not passing judgment, I hope you understand." Then, letter in hand, she reminds him: "In this state, no one's ever been brought to trial without the body."

As Gayle leaves, her things neatly packed in a copy paper box, Ben imagines Mirabelle's body in a velour track suit on weekends before they were married, how he couldn't believe she was his, could come up behind her where she stood pouring cream into her coffee and make her want him the way he wanted her. Though he didn't think about their future, left that to Bella, he had never considered his life at the center of a mystery, only her at the center of his love.

Eloise slips further into dementia. He passes her on the road one day, two goats hanging their heads out the passenger side window of her new sedan. He calls to ask if she needs her pills, but she doesn't answer the phone and doesn't return his messages. When he visits, she opens the door a crack and even then he can smell the filth. She says, "They've got the whole place bugged. Put cameras in the showerhead. You're not safe here anymore."

By May, his severance runs out. He mulches Bella Bride's brilliant rhododendrons at the foot of their driveway. His son toddles about picking up sticks and putting them in his mouth. When Ben takes them from him and suggests he put them in his wagon, the little boy grins, bark slivers on his tongue.

Instead of a neighborhood rising around his family, his street is still trees and gravel piles. If a car drives by, it's usually the detective hoping he'll catch Ben burning bloody sheets or burying a steak knife. Ben doesn't mind the intrusion. He waves, encourages more questions though there aren't any. The builder asks him several times to relocate. Nicely, not so nicely, then downright threatening. He can't describe to this man, to anyone, that he's sure Bella will be back. This is her house, her dream. No telling what she might do if she returns and someone else has moved in.

It's not that he doesn't envision a peaceful place to raise his son, to practice law or stock shelves. He's considered Oregon, drawn to fog and distance. On his good days, it's possible to imagine that there against a grainy sky, sea sounds through his open windows, he might find a friend.

Had some bad luck, he will tell him, relieved that he can say that now.

IT CAN'T BE THIS WAY EVERYWHERE

"It will come about gradually," the doctor had said. "You remember, Daniel, what it was like with your mother?"

"We thought it was her accident," he said. "We thought that's what—damaged—her."

Alzheimer's, Ruth thought, still as marble beside him. Still as if the doctor was speaking to someone else's forty-eight-year-old husband.

Daniel's mother had fallen off a stepladder as she cleaned a light fixture. Her concussion had been so severe, she suffered migraines for years afterward.

"When she started forgetting things, even though she was so young, we just assumed," he said to Ruth later. "She did crossword puzzles. She sent Christmas cards to families they had been stationed with when my father was in the Army and never forgot a street address."

That first month, he catalogued all his memories for her as if to prove everyone wrong—the button missing off his flannel jacket when he was ten, the Estée Lauder Eau de Toilette scent of his first girlfriend's neck, the only line of lyrics his record player skipped over in either of the *Blonde on Blonde* albums. About his illness and what would be required of her, Ruth never said, I can't do this. Other people said it, said that she had many strengths, but she was not even that kind of mother—nurturing, patient. She wasn't cut out to take that kind of care of anyone. It was true, she was not overly compassionate, but she had been an accomplished child in a large family of accomplished children. When she heard she wasn't something, she wanted, more than anything, to be that, to cross it off the list.

Besides, she thought, I haven't had to do anything like this yet. And now that she did, well, they would see.

But first, she had to leave him. She stood in the airport with Daniel whose secretary had to log him into his computer most mornings. His home phone number was taped to the dashboard of his car. He can still get the children home safe, Ruth thought, and keep them that way for a month. She had received the fellowship a year ago. It had been in the works, the money appropriated, the institute expecting her. She and Daniel had come to the decision together, regardless of what anyone else suspected. But she knew what it looked like, her leaving.

The night before she left, Daniel had taken her out to dinner. They had gotten silly on two bottles of expensive champagne and had fumbled through awkward sex in the parking garage afterwards.

"Some scholar," he had whispered in her ear, her head against the concrete piling next to their parked car, and it had made her desperate for him. Immediately afterward, when he couldn't find the keys, it shamed her, the kind of desire she had felt for someone already becoming a child.

"When I told him to check his pocket, he didn't know what I meant, had forgotten what that little thing on his pants was called," Ruth had said to her sister, Margaret.

Margaret said: "And you still got on that plane."

But those four weeks had made little difference in Daniel's health. Once Ruth returned, he welcomed her as if she had been gone overnight.

Now, research completed, she had only to write the book. For the next year at least, she had a job that would allow her to be home.

"I'm going to make borscht," Daniel said, shortly after her arrival. "But I have to get some things at the store."

He left her on the couch beside their nine-year-old, Anna. Ruth thought of asking her daughter if it was okay that he still drove. She wondered if he had gone off on errands like this recently. But Anna had her nose in a book Ruth had not seen, some sort of quiz book she was anxious to share with her mother. She didn't seem concerned that her father had dropped Ruth's bags in the front hall an hour ago and had gone back out for groceries.

"It's simple, Mom," Anna said. "I ask you a question and you answer it."

Ruth settled into the cushions and listened for her younger daughter Isabel singing in the bathtub upstairs.

"Chocolate or vanilla?" Anna asked. Ruth answered: chocolate. Anna tossed more questions at her mother so that Ruth had to consider her favorite movie, the nicest thing she'd done for someone (this took her a few seconds), the best gift she'd ever received.

"Do you play this with Daddy?" Ruth asked.

"Do you know what his best gift ever was?" Anna asked. "Us. You and me and Isabel."

Ruth's response had been a blue ten-speed.

Anna handed her mother the book. "Now, you ask me."

Ruth flipped through the book noting the different girls who had already filled out some pages. She felt relieved that she had the kinds of children who made friends. She had worried that, if her children weren't like that, she would have had no idea how to fix it. She would have been as helpless as she was trying to derail what might already be spinning inside her girls, waiting until they had really accomplished something in their lives, until it was certain they'd passed it onto to their own children, before revealing itself.

"Which would you rather be called: pretty, smart, or sensitive?" Ruth asked. She had to explain that sensitive meant aware of others' feelings.

"Sensitive, then," Anna said, and seemed sad that she might not be.

Ruth had no idea she would find Anna's answer painful, that she would see her daughter's doubt as her own failure. She closed the book and suggested they set the table. "We haven't eaten together in such a long time," she said. "Let's use candles."

Daniel returned shortly after with everything he needed. Ruth had not thought it possible. Even in his healthy days there had always been something he'd forgotten, but he could not recall the name of the soup he was making. Ruth had had to find the recipe for him, and the next morning, she found his razor in his sock drawer when she went to put away clothes.

This is how it will be, she thought, returning the razor to the shelf in their shower. Like a trail of breadcrumbs that I can follow to the complete dissolution of sense.

It was as she stood at the window in the bathroom that she first noticed the cat, a long-haired black animal that dashed across her yard and into the shed where the children's outdoor toys were kept.

The cat came back often that first week, streaking across the yard with a glance towards their windows. The girls were thrilled.

"We've seen it from the bus," Anna said. "Maybe we can catch it."

"It must belong to someone," Ruth said.

"It's a wild one," Isabel said. "Oliver down the street says it lives in his garage sometimes."

"If it's wild, it won't come near humans anyway," Ruth said.

But, cornered in the shed one day when Ruth went for the hose coiled from the fall before, the animal startled her, hissing from its perch on the rafters. Ruth was not an animal lover, had never been close enough to a cat to notice its eyes. This one's were yellow.

That night, Daniel called her from work.

"I'll be late," he said, as if he were lying about something. In the old days, Ruth thought, this is the voice men used when they were having an affair.

"Is everything all right?" she asked.

She had left it up to him to tell his colleagues what was happening, to explain why he had forgotten meetings lately, had misplaced documents, could not recall their names. He would not be in charge of any major projects but could research things as simple as addendums to building codes, could function as part of a site evaluation team, but as a subordinate. He would be supervised by his closest friend, the person responsible for him continuing to work there at all.

Where was Jim now? Ruth thought. Had he gone home already? Been at a client's for the day? She had to consider what might happen when Daniel was alone there.

"I am in the parking garage," Daniel said. "In the car."

"Keys?" Ruth said. "Do you have the keys?"

"I have the keys. But I have no idea how to find you."

That weekend, Ruth sat at her desk. She had never written a book but was finding it easier than she had hoped. Chapter by chapter, she plugged in notes, examples. The process was as manageable as any of the shorter research papers she had published. She followed her outline and it led her, piece by piece, towards a logical conclusion.

When Anna called from outside, Ruth turned to look out the window. Anna cupped something in her hands. An animal of some kind? It was hard to tell. Where was Daniel? Did he know what they were doing? That they could be bitten or scratched? Maybe this marked the point at which he could no longer be alone with the girls even for a few daylight hours outside the room where she sat.

Ruth hurried down the stairs and into the glaring afternoon, hearing, as she squinted into the brightness: "It's a kitten, Mommy. We found them."

In the gloom of the shed, behind a propped-up wheelbarrow, two more kittens huddled over a bit of fur. A fresh kill left by their mother. A fourth kitten lay by itself screeching. All the babies were black with white bibs and socks. They were too young to scamper away or to hiss. Daniel placed one in Isabel's hands, scooped up the others and came out into the light.

"Look, Mom," Isabel said, holding the kitten up. "She has blue eyes."

In the grass, three of them crawled forward, picking up legs as if to free themselves from something sticky. The fourth one turned on its side and continued its piercing cries.

"Maybe we shouldn't touch that one," Ruth suggested. "She seems very afraid."

But the girls ignored her, so absorbed were they in this gift. Ruth acknowledged their discovery the same way: something to keep the girls amused so she could work. What harm could it do to have them play with the creatures for a few hours until the mother cat returned? She was heading back to the house, ideas for the next chapter rushing at her, when Daniel said, "What we'll do is try to trap the mother. There are places that sterilize feral cats for free and raise the kittens."

How could he do this? Have these moments, ribbon-thin, of absolute certainty? They made everything else seem like a mistake, all the expertise and solemn pronouncements, the medical exams that ruled out any other possible causes for his deterioration.

"Imagine this," she had told her sisters after Daniel's CT scan revealed a healthy globe. The women had met at a restaurant Ruth loved that overlooked the harbor, boats in their slips, the bridge between her town and this one opening to allow tall-masted vessels to pass. "We were disappointed that they didn't find a tumor."

"Who are you going to get to take care of him?" Margaret had asked, and their other sisters leaned in as if to hear a secret.

"Who do you think?" she said. "I'm his wife for god's sake."

Margaret continued to stare until Ruth pushed her plate away.

Her other sisters bowed their heads over their own uneaten salads.

Now, Daniel turned to her, a stricken look on his face, and said, "Unless you think it would be too much."

Isabel began to cry, plucking up a kitten and pushing it under Ruth's chin. "Please, Mommy," she said. "We've never had a pet. You've never allowed us."

"It's foolish to cry," Ruth said. "Totally unnecessary."

She recalled the dinner table conversations where a healthy Daniel teased her about getting a dog, but it was true, Ruth had always said no. Too much time, too much responsibility for a woman who felt she spent entirely too much time addressing the needs of others. Now this thought made her laugh out loud. Her daughters stared at her as if she was the one losing her mind.

"We can keep them for a little while," she said. This plan of Daniel's could keep him busy, too. Maybe if he just had something absorbing to do, something that required so little reasoning. "They are in quite a lot of danger out there. From coyotes. Fisher cats. But only until the shelter can pick them up."

Their neighbor, though barely fifty years old, was an old world craftsman who made his living repairing church organs and spent his weekends weaving sea grass into the seats of homemade chairs. How many times, even in less frightening days, had Ruth been relieved that Armando was at home when pipes burst or carpenter ants threatened to gnaw away the eastern wall of their house? She had not had courage enough to share Daniel's diagnosis with anyone outside of family, however. So when Daniel marched across the street in search of a trap for the mother cat, Ruth let him go. Whatever he requested, Armando would provide. In small ways, they could still be saved.

Now, for example, Armando toted the trap over himself.

"Woodchucks ate all my lettuce one summer. I caught a whole family of them in this thing," he said. "Let's hope it still works."

He set the trap up in the shed and baited it with one of the kittens. Pried from its siblings, it protested plaintively. Daniel watched for a few moments, then wondered aloud what he had done with his polka-dotted tie.

"Don't worry about that now," Ruth advised him, her palms prickling. Armando glanced up from his perch on their back deck.

Daniel smiled at them, sun blinking off his glasses. "Right," he said. "Right. Everything is working out just fine."

He repeated this several times before Ruth reminded him they needed to be quiet for the mother cat to come back.

"This must be the same cat who's had kittens up and down the street," Armando said. "A couple litters every summer. The Blivens found her in their garage when they got back from vacation, but by the time they called the shelter, she had moved them. She's been in the Brunelles' tool shed and the Jenkinses' hedges."

Ruth considered how little of anyone else's life she knew about. How, on snowy days, as Armando plowed people's driveways with his tractor or delivered Portuguese fish stew up and down the street, she sat inside hoping the doorbell didn't ring.

"You've had no interest in making friends," her mother commented recently. "And now you're going to need some."

Before Ruth could bristle anew at the critique, the mother cat slunk past them into the shed. Ruth waited for the sound of the trap closing. Instead, the cat ran back out, the baby in her mouth. At this, Ruth and Armando sprinted after her, dodging the Jenkinses' forsythia hedge, lawn chairs, rock garden. The cat, nimble over the same obstacles even with the kitten in her mouth, eluded them until they neared a stone wall, Ruth wondering how they would scale it, Armando several steps behind her, calling to her to forget it, to let this one go.

"You're never going to be able to catch her," he said.

Why did people doubt her? A PhD, two children, a book deal later.

What did it take, really, to convince people you had everything under control? As she sought some foothold to clamber over the stones, she heard meowing and looked down to see the kitten worming its way through the grass. A hundred yards away, the mother glanced back once more before darting off into the woods. Ruth held the kitten against her beating heart. Before they had moved here, she had never seen a fisher cat or a coyote, but now she had seen both, had heard, too, the coyote pack's post-kill yips.

"I saved you," she said, sorry only that she hadn't also saved its mother. When she turned, intending to hold the prize up to Armando, he wasn't looking at her. Instead, he too was turned back, looking towards Daniel who staggered after them, calling her name, crying.

———

Daniel lay upstairs in their bed, the sun across his chest, his arm over his eyes. "She isn't going away," he said.

"Of course I'm not," Ruth said. "I'm not going anywhere."

Downstairs, on the three-season porch off the side of their house, the girls sat cross-legged on the floor and passed the kittens back and forth. Ruth could hear their murmurs, the kittens' cries.

"She isn't running away," Daniel said again, without removing his arm.

When Ruth came downstairs, Armando squatted with the girls. He had brought a stack of newspapers and a box lined with an old towel.

"They'll feel safer in something like this," he said. "You can put it back in the shed with them even."

She hesitated as if to speak, but then decided against it.

"You're not thinking of keeping them?" Armando smiled, as if he already knew the answer to such a silly question.

Ruth stiffened. "We're going to turn them over to the shelter. We have no intention of turning them loose out there."

Armando said nothing, but Ruth knew what he was thinking: Crazy. Let him think it. Sometimes the most compassionate choices were also the most difficult ones to understand.

The first shelter Ruth called, the one that trapped and neutered feral cats according to Daniel, was closed for another two days. The message reminded callers that this was a volunteer operation. Meanwhile, the kittens napped. Were they like human newborns, Ruth wondered, regret twisting in her belly? Hungry often? Awake only to eat?

As she stood on the porch considering what to do next, Isabel looked up from where she kneeled over the box.

"I feel something," she said. "Under my legs."

Ruth felt it, too, a subtle vibration and then heard the low growl that produced it.

"It's the mother," Anna said. "She's underneath us."

The hairs rose on Ruth's arms. Her daughters' faces darkened.

"Will she hurt us?" Isabel asked, rising and stepping onto the threshold where she could no longer feel the tremor. In the box, a kitten stirred and mewed back, its siblings uncurling, too, answering their mother.

"She wants her babies," Anna said. Again, her sister began to cry. "We took her babies."

"Don't be silly," Ruth snapped. "We're saving these kittens from being killed."

But Ruth did consider returning the animals to the shed and letting nature take its course. This mother had every right to threaten them. They had taken something they had no business touching. When Anna stomped her foot, the cat darted back out into the yard. By now, the kittens were inconsolable, climbing over one another in an attempt to escape.

Anna lifted one out and tried to comfort it. "You can't go back out there," she crooned. "It's hard to be separated from your mama, but this is for the best. We just need to figure out what to feed you."

From inside the house, Daniel called: "Kitten formula through an eye dropper. We can get it from any vet."

They found him on the computer, dressed in a dark suit as if he was going to work, the polka-dotted tie knotted perfectly at his neck.

"It also says feral cats are awesome mommies," he told the girls. "They have to be to make it out in the wild."

When Ruth glanced down at the screen, she noticed he was barefoot, that somehow, he had sliced part of his big toe which bled onto the wood floor.

———— • ————

While Daniel sat cross-legged in his suit pants and white shirt, his toe bandaged, showing the girls how to hold the kitten under its chin to feed it, Ruth dialed the number of another shelter, a large no-kill place Armando's wife had suggested over the phone. Frieda had not sounded surprised to hear from Ruth. In fact, she had the information so readily available, Ruth had an idea that once Armando had gotten home and told her what was going on, they had both known their help would be needed. Ruth vowed not to ask them for another thing.

"Just be careful not to press the dropper," Daniel said, his voice soothing, quiet. The girls' heads hovered so closely to the kitten's, Ruth marveled that Daniel could see to feed the baby. "Let the kitty suck just as it would from its mother."

Ruth remembered trying to breastfeed Anna, how surprised she had been at the infant's tenacity. A few days after they left the hospital, her nipples grew so tender, she couldn't cover herself with a sheet. Rather than admit how difficult it was, she counted to ten when Anna latched on, closed her eyes against the pain and told herself it would get easier. A week went by before she admitted this to Daniel who called the midwife.

"You have thrush," he told her, in the same voice he now used with the girls. "It isn't anything you did wrong." Then, he traveled to a holistic practitioner to buy a paste she applied to her nipples and to her baby's mouth. Cured her.

When Ruth had maneuvered through all the shelter's voice prompts and was rewarded by a human voice, she turned from the tableau of Daniel and her daughters and cleared her throat.

"The mother abandoned them?" the woman asked. She sounded suspicious, not what Ruth had anticipated. Ruth felt justified lying to her. "And you think they're how old?"

Ruth had no idea but she said they had been eating meat when the girls found them.

"They were eating meat but there was no mother around? You waited to make sure?"

"We haven't seen any cat for days," Ruth said.

The woman sighed. "And you're positive they'll let you hold them? Because if feral kittens are too old, they're impossible to tame and we would not, under any circumstances, be equipped to handle them."

"My children are feeding them now," Ruth said, her anger rising. "So I'm sure you'll be *equipped* to handle the situation." She wanted to scream this into the phone, but understood that getting rid of these animals might not be as easy as she had hoped.

The woman stayed silent for a moment. "We can take them Tuesday," she said. Three days away. "Bring them in a crate, and if for any reason you have to cancel, please let us know. We're very busy here."

Ruth snorted. "I'm sure you think so."

When Margaret called, she told Ruth she was crazy. "Why on earth would you take that on?"

"It's a good lesson for the girls," Ruth said. "And it was the right thing to do."

"There were days, you know, when people put a litter of kittens into a plastic bag with a rock and dropped them into a quarry."

"There were days when Christians were fed to lions as well, and when it was okay to beat your wife. The list of accepted barbarisms goes on and on."

"All I'm saying is that it isn't the worst thing in the world to let wild kittens be wild. Especially when you have two young children, a book contract and an ill husband. Honestly, Ruthann, what are you proving?"

After dinner, Daniel grew angry when Ruth reminded him it was time to feed the kittens. He had been scratched earlier, he said. From that fussy little one who never stopped meowing. He had ruined a perfectly good white shirt. The girls stared at him, Isabel tearing up, Anna patting her hand.

"I can help," Ruth said. "Anna will teach me."

"You should help," Daniel snapped. "I am all alone here and I don't want to be hurt again. There's something terribly wrong with that animal." He tossed a glass into the sink and it shattered which made him curse.

Ruth sent the girls onto the porch with the rag and the eyedropper. "I'll warm up the formula and be right there," she said, though she had not written a word since that morning and had hoped to commit a couple hours that night to her work. Her hands shook as she moved him away from the sink. She should hold him, she knew. She had learned from his doctor that he might need to be comforted during more fearful moments, but he stunk of sour formula, his own sweat and something else she couldn't name, decay, dead flesh. She put her arm on his shoulder.

"You are not alone," she said, "even though it might feel like that. I am always going to be here."

He raised his eyebrows. "You? You left months ago. On an airplane and we had no idea where you'd gone."

"You forgot that I was going to Stockholm. And that I called every day. But that's okay because from now on, I'm not going anywhere. I can take care of the kittens so they won't hurt you again."

"You don't even like cats," he said, shaking his head and laughing bitterly as he began picking up the shards of glass. "And you were running away like a maniac just a few hours ago, but that man caught you."

———

As Ruth filled the dropper for the last kitten, she spoke to her daughters about what they had just witnessed. "Remember what I told you? That Daddy has a sickness in his brain? Well, that's why he acts that way. You shouldn't cry about it. It's silly to think he would ever hurt you."

Both girls listened but offered nothing. They bathed the other animals with warm washcloths and set them in a box that Daniel had filled with shredded newspaper. A makeshift litter box, he said. It worked. Ruth reached for the final kitten which, instead of its usual whining, was mostly silent. When she lifted it to her face, she gagged. It was the stench she had smelled on Daniel. She set the animal down and drew back.

"Something's wrong with this one," she said. The animal did not lay flat but tilted its tiny body to the side. When she examined it, she saw maggots squirming in a wound no bigger than a fingernail clipping. She turned her head away and dry heaved.

"What is it, Mommy?" Anna asked. Isabel shivered.

"I think it's time to bring the kittens back to their mother," Ruth said, immediately feeling how liberating that would be. The ease of the solution stunned her. "We can't do this. I was wrong to think we could."

Isabel bowed her head, sniffling onto the front of her shirt.

Anna looked wildly from her sister to her mother. "But you said they'd be killed out there. That it is a terrible life for them. You said coyotes would eat them."

This intensified Isabel's grief and brought Daniel out onto the porch.

"Mommy says we have to put them back," Isabel said, desperate. "They have to go back out there." No moon shone. The little girls peered out into the blackness. When Anna looped her arm around her sister, Daniel turned on Ruth.

"What is wrong with you?" he said. "First you say we'll rescue them, now you change your mind?"

"You don't want to help anymore, either, Daniel," she said, feeling as if this was familiar ground: a score-keeping argument with the man she married, someone infinitely capable of defending himself. "You throw a tantrum and walk away from the responsibility. I have enough to take care of enough without worrying about some sick thing that's going to die no matter what we do."

The girls told them to stop. The kittens clawed at the insides of their box. Daniel squatted beside his daughters and shushed them, one hand on each girl's shoulder.

"It's a lot of work, taking care of these kittens," he said. He spoke so softly, they had to quiet themselves to hear him. "But we're going to do this because it's the right thing to do. We are helping creatures who can't help themselves. We took something on and we have to see it through no matter how difficult it gets."

Isabel buried her head in his shoulder. Anna rubbed her hand softly over a kitten's back.

"We're going to go upstairs to read together and then I'll come down and take care of the sick kitty," Daniel said. Over his shoulder, Isabel stared dully at her mother. Anna nodded her head as if finally someone was speaking sense, then she took her father's hand.

"But you said wild cats are the best mommies," Isabel said as they moved inside. "Why would she let her baby get hurt like that?"

"She had to hunt," Daniel said. "She had to keep herself strong so she could feed them. Even a good mommy like that can't always be there to protect her babies. Your mommy left, too. Remember?"

Ruth wanted to walk away, to see how far Daniel could get with this newest problem, but even more importantly, she wanted to take care of it herself, to show her daughters she would not abandon this project no matter how idiotic it had been to take it on.

Over the telephone, the on-call vet told Ruth the situation was hopeless. "A kitten that young whose flesh is already dead doesn't stand a chance; euthanasia is really the only viable option." She spoke so kindly, Ruth had to sit down. She longed to keep her on the phone, this one capable voice. "You can bring her into Boston tonight," the vet continued. "Angel Memorial is open twenty four hours, or you could wait until tomorrow morning, but she'll most likely be gone by then."

Ruth recalled Daniel's earlier agitation. She had left him for four weeks. What could one trip to the animal hospital—a few hours total—be compared with that? But he had become so paranoid about her leaving and it was so quiet upstairs. He must have fallen asleep beside the girls. To wake him would risk him being disoriented or still angry. The kitten was a wild animal, one that surely would have died despite their interference no matter what Daniel told their children. She would not leave merely to hurry along the inevitable.

When she hung up, Ruth considered bathing the wound, giving the kitten some comfort, but she couldn't bear to touch it. She had placed it in a shoebox alone and had walked away, willing herself not to think about what the animal might be enduring. Instead, she stripped off the clothes she had worn when she had attempted to feed it and tossed them into the washing machine then retreated upstairs to write. So grateful was she for the concrete nature of her task that the words came effortlessly. She didn't look up until it was almost midnight. Without glancing in the smaller box, Ruth fed the healthy kittens, wiped the milk from their faces and necks, let them crawl through the litter box and then put them away for the night.

In the laundry room, she bent to shove the clothes into the dryer, her head near the screen of an open window. It took her a moment to hear the growl, so low in the throat it was. The cat perched on a sill so close Ruth could have reached out and touched it if the screen had not been in place. She saw nothing but light reflecting off the yellow orbs before the cat leapt off the sill and disappeared, full of useless milk.

Outside, Ruth set the tiny box in the grass, covered the kitten with an old t-shirt of Isabel's that was paint-stained, torn on one sleeve. "Come back for her," Ruth said aloud and felt a relief that surprised her so, she had trouble walking back to the house.

In the morning, Daniel leaned over Ruth and asked about his polka-dotted tie.

"I haven't seen it since you wore it yesterday," she told him. She had been up every two hours, tending to the animals. Her face felt swollen, her head hurt.

The bed sank beneath his weight. When she looked up, she found him sitting with his head in his hands. "Have you even tried to find it?" he asked.

"I couldn't because I was busy with the kittens," she said.

He looked confused. "Kittens?"

Ruth tossed off the covers, exposing the lower half of her body where her nightgown had risen. When Daniel looked up, his expression changed. It was not desire Ruth saw in his face, but something more primal. Frightened, she pulled her robe off the end of the bed and wrapped herself in it.

"I hear the girls," she said, but as she walked by him, he reached out and grabbed her wrist, slid his hand up her thigh. She pulled away.

The girls knelt over the box. Isabel sucked the ends of her hair, a habit Ruth thought they had cured her of. Anna re-arranged the kittens, searching for the missing one. Which one of her girls would succumb the way Daniel had, to a disease that had been with him since birth? What had they done, she and Daniel, when they had decided to have children? How could they not have known all that they might subject them to?

"She isn't in there," Ruth said, as if it hadn't become clear. "I put her outside so her mother could take care of her. She's too ill for us to help her."

"But what if her mother didn't come?" Anna asked, simultaneously drawing her sister's hair away from her mouth. Ruth expected her to call for her father, but she stared at Ruth, suspicious. "We have to make sure."

The box was where Ruth had left it beside a hydrangea heavy-headed with blossoms. Bees murmured. Flies lit on the undisturbed rag that had been Isabel's shirt. The little girl cried out when she saw it, forgetting they had relegated it to the rag drawer. Ruth knew before she drew back the cloth that the mother had not come, or that, if she had, she had also known that there was nothing to be done for something so impaired. The kitten's body was stiff, her mouth open in a grimace of amazingly tiny teeth. At least no other animal had disturbed her as she lay dying.

"I knew her mother wouldn't come," Anna said, emotionless. Isabel wept into the crook of her bare arm.

Ruth closed her eyes, breathed in the scent of Armando's newly mulched bushes, his freshly mown grass.

"There are some things we can't fix, Anna," she said, her voice dispassionate. "But we'll give her a funeral, if you like. We'll make it very special."

Daniel had been uncertain which tool to use to dig the hole. When Anna handed him the pointed shovel, he nodded. He trusted her, that was clear from the way he took what she offered him, but he studied the tool, ran his hand along the handle, before it occurred to him what his task must be. He dug a small hole beneath the uneven shade of the hydrangeas. Anna gripped her sister's hand. Ruth held the box, far enough away so that she couldn't catch the stench. In two days, they would drive together to leave the other kittens at the shelter where people would take this burden from them. Her sister would have to admit: Ruth was more capable than she thought.

I did the right thing, Ruth told herself as she stood over the tiny grave. I have taught my daughters a lesson in responsibility, in loss. One day no matter that the names of their loved ones would escape them, they would remember the details of this day as vividly as their father recalled his own childhood.

When the hole was complete, a square so true, it hurt Ruth to see it, Daniel looked up at her.

"I did it," he said.

Anna suggested they all say something nice about the kitten.

"She was the prettiest of all the kittens," Isabel said.

Anna added: "She was a very brave kitten who would have made a wonderful pet for someone if only she had lived long enough."

When the girls finished, they looked to their mother who could think of nothing to add. Instead, she stooped to lower the box, dipping her head beneath the showy blooms. As she did so, she heard a sound so small, it might have been a strangled meow, or the far-off call of a bird, or nothing at all. Could the kitten be alive after all? It had already taken so long to die, had already spent so much time pricking Ruth's conscience. She envisioned the only life available to this creature, the suffering Ruth had no answers for. Even if it was alive, what would be the point of saying so? The end was unalterable. She stepped into the shadows beside her husband and placed the box in its perfect hole.

"Go ahead," she said to Daniel, who leaned onto his shovel staring into the grave.

He was humming, something Ruth had never heard him do. When he looked up, she motioned to the shovel and he shook his head as if his forgetfulness was funny. One shovelful was enough to cover the box. But Daniel continued working until it had been completely filled in, more than a foot of dirt pressing down on the insubstantial container. What would people think, Ruth thought, if they knew what she heard and what she had done anyway? And how could she have explained what she knew without the accompanying judgment: even buried alive, the poor animal was better off.

HAVING YOUR ITALY

In the beginning, when we talked on the phone as strangers, we said everything simply.

"What would you do if you won a million dollars?" you asked.

"Buy cows," I said. Because I grew up on a farm, I told you.

You would take piano lessons. Because you used to play the trumpet.

Much later, I told you how my father's hands swelled so in winter, I had to tie his shoes when he went to funerals and that going to funerals was the only time he left his work. I told you how, the morning of his own funeral, I went out alone to do the chores, found his jackknife on the windowsill over some bales of hay where he'd left it the day before, picked it up, expecting it to be warm the way it was whenever he handed it to me.

You told me you left the trumpet in the closet of the bedroom you had had as a child. You had devoted yourself to your high school jazz band, but now the trumpet wasn't the only thing you didn't have time for. There was scuba diving, sea kayaking, meeting your best friend for a beer. Time to talk about things like the time he broke your nose playing mud football and knew enough about you to fill out the emergency room forms.

At your favorite pizza place, we sat at a lacquered table. You turned up the edges of the placemat, folding tiny triangles into each corner of the map of Italy.

"Let's buy a house on Block Island," you said. "You could write a romance novel and make lots of money. Then we could afford to live near the ocean."

"What would you do?" I asked.

"I'd repair small engines."

Over your head hung a picture of Jack and Bobby Kennedy.

"I don't know how to write romance novels and you don't know anything about small engines."

The artist had painted JFK in profile. Robert, in the background, faced forward. Sometimes, people asked me where I was when Kennedy was shot. I was nine months old. Your mother was two babies away from having you. I couldn't help feeling we'd missed something together.

"Isn't there someplace you imagine yourself living?" you said.

I did then—when you suggested it. Then I could picture myself on the second floor of a Cape with natural shingles and a dusting of salt on the windowpanes, computer keys clicking over the sounds of the ocean.

"I thought we were moving to Italy," I said.

That's what you suggested some mornings while you made pancakes out of whatever you found in the pantry: peanuts, bananas, raspberry preserves. We would open a breakfast place, American style, in Florence. That early in the day, fine parentheses framed your mouth. I told you Italians don't eat big breakfasts, but you were convinced that others, no matter what their cultural background, would be as intrigued by novelty as you were. You ladled the batter onto the hot pan before slicing bananas into the pancakes. A secret, you said, of your success. A thin crust formed around the edges, a filigreed edge that tasted of iron.

In the pizza parlor, as I waited for your response, the waitress put a pitcher of dark beer in front of us and you poured it, tilting my glass over the Mediterranean.

"We will," you said. "Go to Italy."

You looked away as if you could see it from here, the small boot testing murky waters with its toe.

In August, we went to Maine. On the way to Acadia, we put the top down and drove inland, away from traffic. You traced routes along one of the maps you brought. I tried to teach you the different breeds of cows.

I pointed to a herd of Herefords, their white faces lifted beyond the barbed wire as we sped by.

"Heifers," you said.

You did well with generalities.

"All young females are heifers."

"Okay, Guernseys."

I told you there were rarely Guernseys in New England now, safer to guess any other breed. Guernseys were the products of people's homesickness maybe, the sentimental choice for a herd, but not animals that could sustain you through long winters, wet springs. Before you could guess again, the next pasture boasted the honey and white of them, the delicate freckles of them on green pasture.

I pulled over. There was no smugness in you, just delight, as if you knew it could work out this way. You smiled at me, at the scene. The map rustled a bit in the breeze and you rested your hand on it without looking away.

That night, we laid a blanket along a crescent of shore and practiced the constellations.

"If we find the Big Dipper, we can find the North Star," I said.

I held my finger up, tracing the outline, thinking you could see it, too.

"I would like looking out the window and seeing cows," you said. "If you want a farm someday. I would like that."

I let my arm fall back into the cool sand but kept my focus on the constellation. "Maybe you need to take one thing off your list and do it."

You flattened out the blanket where it had wrinkled between our faces and watched me.

"Just one thing on the list so you know you can do it," I said. "Like Italy was for me. The thing I'd always wanted to do without knowing how I'd do it. I had a piece of paper from a friend of a friend. It told me to get off the train in Venice and take a left. I did it. I took the left. And it didn't make me stop wanting things. It just made me understand I can have them."

"Well," you said, "I haven't had my Italy."

———

You brought me to bars in New Haven and ordered pitchers of locally brewed ales, porters and stouts. This was long before brew houses with their exposed kegs and their bags of malt slumping against the walls became popular.

You waited for me to taste a mouthful, then said, "Isn't it good? Isn't it better?"

I didn't know what to compare it to. I taught myself to drink beer in college because it was cheap. It took years for me to look forward to a cold beer on a hot day.

This tasted like coffee. "It's different."

"But do you like it?" you said, and I said yes because it meant something to you to have me admit it.

When you decided to brew your own beer, I went along for the ride to the International Food Emporium, a place you found in the phone book.

"We could make this our business," you said. "You could design some labels, pick a name. We'd start small, stay up all night brewing and go to work tired the next day, knowing those jobs were temporary."

We sat with those ideas between us.

Spring was gray as granite that year. We didn't bother getting directions since the destination itself could not be our adventure.

"We'll feel our way around," you said, and I sat there with your amazement for a few wrong exits before we stumbled upon what we were looking for. I remember the rain mottling light through the windshield, how beautiful your face was, how I studied it the way I studied paintings, the view off a balcony of a place I'd never been before.

The Food Emporium was a soggy, squat building where water ran over peeling clapboards. Inside were scents of burlap and vinegar, salted ham and a month of rain. You approached the only other person there, a woman whose scalp peeled visibly beneath wiry red and gray hairs. I examined the shelves stacked as miscellaneously as some kitchen cabinets: one box of pancake mix supporting a bag of lentils, two cans of Green Giant corn and a box of birthday candles, the cellophane torn. Amidst the familiar, there were curries and fennel powder, anise, vanilla beans. One deli case housed imported cheeses, jars of black olives; the other, souvenir back scratchers from Connecticut.

You handled a bag of hops, trying the pellets with your fingertips as the woman gave you instructions. I found a section reserved for cemetery statues—shelves and shelves of Virgin Marys and saints who stared beatifically at their feet.

"Hold these," you said, handing me a bag of dried apricots, "and I'll buy you a bishop confirming a lost soul."

I had been thinking about something, but I couldn't remember what, only that I had felt far away. That it was a surprise to be called back.

"North Star Brewers." When you looked at me, I said: "The name."

"That's good. You came up with something just like that."

But it hadn't really happened that quickly. The articulation of my own dream.

The woman came out of the back room carrying a glass jar and a funnel. I put the apricots back on a shelf velveted with dust and helped you carry everything to the car.

The day darkened on our way home, darkened the way early spring does in Connecticut. Remember that? Remember how silky dusk was over the naked forsythias trying so hard to be new? Remember how you showed me old railway bridges before it got too dark, how you saw some mystery in the skeletal rust of them?

I remember that afternoon, the stubborn bushes separating opposite directions, the starkness of railway bridges no one used anymore. I remember the day fading on that highway, the way days fade in a new spring, the way days fade when it rains, the way days fade.

WEIGHT

Todd and Jonas buy me a wind-up alarm clock because they don't want me sleeping beside the digital one.

"They give you brain tumors," Todd says. "Imagine being in danger when you're at your most defenseless. That is, if you're sleeping. If you can sleep."

I can't. Not in that bed, not in the chair by the cold fireplace, not at the kitchen table beneath the unlit chandelier I'd gotten at a yard sale when I stopped for things like that, things glinting on the side of the road.

"It's better for staring at, too," Jonas says.

They come in without knocking now, scold me for leaving the door unlocked.

"Isn't that why we live here? Serenity? A false sense of security?" I say. It is why I moved here though Todd says they moved next door, two years later, because they thought it would be romantic.

"Well," Jonas says. "You're not so grief-stricken that you can't be snarky. That's a good sign."

Four months after my lover died, Jonas and Todd are the only people I think are funny. They do things no one else does, say what isn't expected. They could have sent another casserole I wouldn't eat. Instead, they buy me a vintage alarm clock and suggest we order pizza.

Maybe when the sun sets in an hour, I will be able to concentrate on a book or a television program. I want pizza, and knowing that feels good, but then Jonas setting out paper plates and Todd cracking ice cubes into glasses makes my throat hurt. The familiarity of their actions, the demands of everyday tasks. I imagine them in their own house thinking of ways to help.

The phone at the pizza place is busy. I hit redial. Busy. When I've finally decided: I want pizza. When Todd has poured our glasses full of the homemade rootbeer he has bought especially for the occasion. I hurl the phone across the room and hit the open window.

Jonas studies the intact screen. "That settles it," he says. "We're getting out of here. We'll stay with my brother in Connecticut. He'll drive us into the city."

"He's a terrible driver," Todd says. He sets the phone on its cradle, re-sets it. Contemplates it. "You should be honest with her, Jonas. He takes risks."

"Enough, old woman," Jonas tells him. Then he says to me: "You know we wouldn't let anything happen to you. You need the city. Time may heal but not without distractions."

"Do you want to go?" Todd says. "Only if you want to go."

Jonas and Todd have the same view out their back windows: a patch of grass and then a reedy spot between us and the mild ascent of foothills, forest. Miles away, the Berkshires rise, blue gray from a dark swatch of pines. What do I want? Whatever it is makes itself known with something as small as a sound, a reflection on the periphery, disappears when I turn to see it. I shrug.

"It will be good to get away from all these trees," Todd says, for all of us.

"Bye bye, little town in a valley," Jonas says. "Hello bright lights."

He puts his arm around me and for a moment I think he might hug me which would embarrass us both; he isn't the type. Instead, he pats my shoulder. He's not much taller than I am, his hair thinning on a pale scalp. He wears sneakers and bright white socks everywhere.

"We'll dine out," he says.

Todd says, "Only, please, no shellfish." He's allergic. "Unless you want it, sweetie."

"You don't have to be generous just because my lover died young and unexpectedly," I say.

Though Todd is always generous with me, Todd who won't stand up straight from years of being the tallest boy in class. As if he wouldn't have stood out enough, with his soft voice, the way he has of touching his face as he listens. I've caused him to fidget with an invisible blemish on his jaw. He casts his eyes down and Jonas sighs.

"If it feels good to say it out loud, then say it out loud," Jonas says. "You lost your lover young and tragically. And you, Todd, don't go getting your feelings hurt."

At least crying because I've hurt someone's feeling is a finite experience. That kind of guilt ebbs. Grief is more a physical presence, brooding and solid, than a feeling. It's a life-sized bronze statue I lug to bed, to the grocery store, to the mailbox. It must be visible. It must be capable of being carted off or left behind.

———

Jonas's brother Will is tall as an oarsman, equal parts warm and surly, with an alarmingly wide smile that caught me off guard when he first flashed it. I've found it difficult to speak ever since. It's desire, uninvited, a visitor so ridiculous, I could laugh out loud. Will takes the wine bottle from me and eases out the cork.

"Shall I pour?" he asks. I nod, take the glasses from Jonas who is suddenly at my side, pushing his brother away.

"We'll take it from here," he says.

Will gets back to cooking. When he leans across the island with broccoli speared on a fork and says: "Try it," I eat from him.

Jonas flicks the burner off and says, "Dinner's ready. We don't want our vegetables mushy."

"Destroys nutrients," Todd says, bent almost in half over the table, one hand behind his back, one hand re-arranging silverware.

Will lights candles, moves them surface to surface, tries one lamp then another until he gets the atmosphere right, checking my face to be sure. I stand as still as if he's painting my portrait. I know what words get said in these first few moments. I know how to exchange smiles. But I don't, and he moves on, refilling wine glasses, pulling out my chair.

We finish our wine on the deck, Todd and I on chaise lounges, Jonas and Will at our feet. A freighter's lights glow offshore. Jonas tells us freighters helped us win World War II.

"Not submarines?" Todd asks, though he doesn't seem interested.

"The obvious is never what saves us," Jonas says.

In the dark, Will touches my ankle: "You have a scar here."

I have been touched there before, the small bowl of tan-less skin rimming ankle bone, that exact spot, and I have been asked: Where did this come from? The idea of giving away even this little bit exhausts me, but Will doesn't ask, just leaves his finger there longer than anyone else has.

Jonas and Todd turn.

"Well." Jonas stands. "We'll need our rest for tomorrow."

Todd says, still watching us, "Maybe just a few more minutes," but Jonas is already holding out his hand to raise him to his feet.

Will shares this house with a man who is rarely home. I lie awake in that strange man's bed, my head surrounded by long panes of a bay window. There's a candle burned to a nub on the nightstand, massage oil, a silver music triangle with its wand. People make love here. And music. Space-clearing music. I won't need any of this for lovemaking, for sex: the stars out the window, the props for intimacy. I will close my eyes, accept the faceless dark.

Next time.

It's the first time I've said that.

In the morning, Jonas is on the deck again where sunlight reveals sailboats and skiffs slicing along the sea's surface.

He hands me his coffee.

"If I have any more of this, boats won't be the only thing racing along pell-mell," he says.

I sip from his cup, the coffee cool and sweet. We sit for a long while in silence. Then Jonas says, "You don't have to tell me about all the ways a man can fill you up."

"I don't feel hollow," I say. "I feel as full as if someone has opened up my head and filled me with cement."

"Even now?"

"I'm wishing for one of those flying dreams. Where you can lift yourself out of a situation just before some danger does you in, but then you realize it's not just to save yourself? It's fun, too. Magical."

"You're not alone with those foothills, you know," he says. "Todd and I aren't ever going to leave you."

"If I had had doting parents, is that the kind of thing they would have said to me?"

"If I had had doting parents, I'd be able to answer that."

Jonas lays his head back in the chaise and closes his eyes. The sun gilds his hair until he appears aged. I cover his hand with mine and look away.

"I worry about you," he says. "My brother's not known for his long commitments. I'm sorry that we brought you here."

"I'm not holding you responsible, Jonas. This isn't about love anyway. Even if I could love him, it's not why I'm glad we came."

"The weight," he says. "It's fear, isn't it? Not what if something happens to him, right? But also, but mostly: how will I handle it? You know, the old what's going to happen to me?"

"Yes," I say. "It's a lot more about fear. Fear of what that next thing will feel like and how you will receive it. How you will add that to everything else."

———

Will drives fast along the Merritt Parkway. Jonas and Todd sit in the back and remind me to buckle my seatbelt. Will sings the lyrics to songs I don't recognize. Every song sounds angry and he scowls, but when the song is over, he points out landmarks as if it's show and tell and we're all here for a tour of his commute. We park in a garage beneath the building where Will works, take the subway to Battery Park.

Ferried out to Ellis Island, Will and I lean against the railing. On a bench behind us, Jonas consults a guidebook. Todd applies sunscreen.

"I've never broken a bone," Will admits, and neither have I. But I like the idea of it. Here it has snapped and here is how we put it together and here is how long it will take to heal.

Jonas says he'll read to us.

"Here's your hat," Todd says.

"Oh right. First I must protect the dome." Jonas shares details of steamship bowels, of immigrants sitting in filthy bunks practicing answers in English: How much money do you have? Who's the president? What's your name?

"Think of how much they couldn't communicate," Todd says.

In the museum, Will considers wall plaques and photographs, reads over people's heads. He moves as if he is without anyone else's history attached to him. Or maybe it's the grace you possess when you haven't had to decide what to do with a story that has an ending and doesn't.

When he catches me watching him, he smiles. Though I want his attention, I don't smile back. It feels like flirting, like adolescence, and I wish, instead, there was a different way to start this time. A way we could skip the beginning.

In the infirmary, I separate and study the gynecological tools. My grandmothers might have been examined by this speculum. This very one. As young girls from Naples, as virgins. It's not just my dread that throbs here, but remnants of their own, these girls powerless to predict what would happen to them, where they would go when they had been funneled through this place. They remembered nothing of their journeys. Or if they did, they chose not to relive them by answering our questions about them.

Their homesickness was also the longing for something that they could never have back. They stepped here into a contract for both worlds. Did they hope they would return to places where they knew street names without street signs, genealogies several generations long without ever learning how to write their own names? They embarked unprepared for the misery of the voyage, but once they understood what suffering separated them from their loved ones, would they have entertained the idea of return? For the familiar, would they have made themselves wretched again? Neither of them did return. They moved to one of three streets in town that were full of Italians. They were not bitter women, my grandmothers, but they never learned English, never fed their children what other kids ate. They packed the kinds of trunks we'd seen in another exhibit here. Polenta pans, spices, a straining cloth for cheeses, eggplant and squash seeds. Set up home somewhere else, they must have thought, but fill it with the recognizable, make it grow what you will eat.

I don't want to see any more. Without looking around for the others, I go outside and sit on a bench. When they find me an hour later, Jonas reprimands me for going off.

"It's the city," he says. "We're not in Kansas anymore."

"It is more like a memorial than I thought," Todd says. "Maybe we should have done Broadway."

"Don't be insane," Will snaps. "It's a beautiful day."

Todd looks away and I look, too, towards where whitecaps froth on the water's surface. The city rises in a shimmering haze.

Jonas waves his arm at the scene: "Lady and gentlemen," he says. "Welcome to the New World."

We get off the ferry and walk without looking at anything, without stopping. I trail behind, tired of talk. Only Todd pauses at shop windows, mulls sausages, men's shoes, glass bulbs that cast rainbows. Will and Jonas lead, Jonas making sense of this neighborhood through its architecture, this square by its memorial garden. He can never be abandoned in a city whose history he knows. He can never be so completely lost that he can't recall something he has read, some fact or episode that he recalls when he sees it fleshed out before him.

But it is Will who guides us so effortlessly we never stop to get our bearings. I follow, content to go unnoticed by the people who have brought me here and the people who pass by.

When we finally stop, it is at an outdoor cafe for an early dinner.

Will says to me, "We'll share a salad first."

When it arrives in front of me, I push it between us. When I can't finish it, he does.

Back at his house, I say goodnight. Hours later, Will pauses outside my door, moves away.

In the morning, we go to a clip of shore behind the house. Will swims out to sailboats on moorings, swims and swims. Jonas reads a Churchill biography; Todd sips water and considers his toes. No one says Will's too far out. His powerful strokes remind me that people drown only when they panic. Todd reaches a long arm out and tilts the umbrella over me without my asking for it and Jonas says, "Good idea," from beneath his hat brim.

Will hangs off a red hull two hundred yards away.

"We have to go soon," Jonas says, watching me over the pages of his book.

I consider the table inside my front door with mail, unsorted for days, phone messages on the backs of envelopes—*call back, call soon, call if,* the staircase risers scuffed from all those trips, the light switch smudged from my groping.

It's true you can feel someone with you even after he's gone, hairs rising on one arm, waking up when someone in an empty house calls your name, the feeling of being closely followed through dimly lit hallways, the scent of woodsmoke on flannel that floats by you in a garishly bright kitchen.

Will is too far out to hear me say, "I'm going to stay here."

———

November. Jonas calls me at Will's and reads a story about a couple who was kidnapped because they slipped into the back seat of the wrong car.

"They thought it was a taxi," he says. "Their bodies were found in a dump."

"But that was in Colombia," I say.

"Still," Jonas says. "One little mistake."

Todd in the background: "Do you know how much trash they compact in one hour in New York?"

"He has a perfectly nice house by the water," Jonas says. "Why you two are always in the city is a mystery. You, of all people. Miss Barefoot-in-the-Grass-and-Snow. Miss Leave-the-Door-Unlocked-and-Keep-the-Porch-Light-Burning-for-Any-Old-Home-Invader."

We go to the city because I ask Will to take me. I request nothing else, and because of this, because of many things, he indulges me.

"You used to be more demanding," Jonas reminds me. "You were always so dependable that way."

Later, sliding against Will in the back seat of a gypsy cab, I ask: "How do you know this car's the real thing?"

Will says, "Here, here, here," to the driver. He repeats many things three times, like my name when he comes. He is impatient with cab drivers, also with waiters and beggars and coat check people. It's the only thing that makes me want to stay home, but no one notices one more rude person in the city. Maybe, I think, I can get used to anything.

"You don't have to know because I do," he says, with his eye near the corner of my eye. The way fish figure each other out.

I only ask out of curiosity and out of respect for Jonas. I have no concern for our safety. We'll arrive. We won't be slaughtered and left at a landfill. If one bad thing happens to you, incredibly bad, unbearably bad, what are the chances something similar will occur?

Jonas also asks if I think this is a good idea, this relationship so soon after. No one ever says so soon after what.

"What shall I wait for?" I ask him.

He thinks I mean how long should I wait, but I mean, what will it feel like? To know when you are finally ready for whatever else is going to happen?

We meet Will's friends in a bar. He introduces me, but maybe they don't hear him. The reunion is chaotic, half-hugs, greetings. Years ago, before his company secured an apartment in the upper West Side, Will stayed with Tara, the only other woman in our group. They slept in the same bed without incident, he says. It doesn't matter. He might have loved her. Or he might have slept with her without love. Thought about it. Wished for it. What would any of it have to do with me? Tara's apartment was so tiny, it had a bathtub in the kitchen so Will bathed while she figured out the coffee machine. You had to dunk under water to wash your hair, he told me. Dunk again to rinse it. When he says this, I see him rising through his own bubbles, blowing naked on weak coffee, his towel draped over the doorframe.

Now I stand with Tara in this bar and say nothing, feel no pressure to speak. I have trouble finding anything to talk about lately and when I do attempt conversation, I'm out of practice.

"Have you met his old girlfriend, Hildie?" Tara asks. "You'd like her."

Will's near the door helping a prostitute find her shoe.

"You would like my dead boyfriend, too," I tell her.

You think jealousy is big, I think of telling Tara. Love? Hate? Paranoia? Come back when you have something really heavy for me to haul around.

She goes to the bathroom.

I can't distinguish Will's friends from strangers. When Cole says hello, he has to reintroduce himself.

"We met when you came in," he says.

"I'm not good with names," I tell him. "Or faces."

But the truth is, I am. Had been.

Cole is reading the same book I have on the nightstand at Will's house. He knows the trick about suspending a wedding ring over a pregnant belly to determine the baby's sex. He spent summers at the beach in the town where I grew up. Things I might have confused for intimacy just the spring before. Now I see them as the kind of filaments that would link us to anyone we meet. If we took the time to discover them. With Will, they emerged more slowly: the unbroken bones, the preferred taste of slightly burned toast, the necessity of quiet talk during lovemaking, his questions, my one word answers. With Cole, the similarities immediately rise to the surface. But even that doesn't make me claim a connection with him more rare than I have with anyone else. Coincidence is not the same as fate. No one knows me here, in a city where I can't escape shoulders and hips and low slung purses. It's why I beg to come as often as I do.

"When you're ready to leave," Cole says, "I'll drive you."

"I'm ready," I say, a little drunk. I hadn't considered going home until he offers and then I want to more than anything.

He has a red car, two-seater. We get in without saying good-bye. At the last minute, Will climbs in and buckles himself into the seat with me. He gives directions, leaning into me heavily around corners. He gets us lost on purpose and though I feel guilty for almost leaving him and then annoyed at his finding us, this makes me laugh. Cole is angry. He drives masterfully, fast, but sure-handed, fearless, but not with the kind of disregard Will has for what's possible.

We end up at Will's company's apartment. Tara and the others wait for us in the lobby.

"What took you so long?" Tara asks. She's folded her arms, stands with two other men I don't recognize. "You invite us to stay over, then you leave us waiting out here?"

Will and I sleep in the bedroom, the others on rugs and couches outside our door. Our room has twin beds. In the one we share, Will tells me Cole thinks I'm beautiful.

"I never told him you were beautiful," Will says. "I surprised him."

I mull the uselessness of my own looks. When I need something badly, such qualities offer no assistance. Though I appreciate the pale planes of Will's chest as he lowers it onto me.

The next morning, Cole sits on our bed where Will and I are naked beneath the sheet, Will curled behind me.

"I have to leave early," Cole says. "But I wanted to see you."

He's showered and smells like hotel soap. His hair is cropped close, a little boy's cowlick where, if he had them, part of his bangs would stick up like otherwise flat water flowing over a reed. He's slender as a boy, too, but with a deep voice, a radio announcer's voice, and he's off to jump out of an airplane somewhere. What if I had met him first? Would he have been proof of the hypothesis that we aren't destined for one true love, that we are creatures, instead, of convenience? Or truth of a new theory: that it is impossible to love only one person at a time?

Cole says, "I wanted to tell you how sorry I am about your old boyfriend. I didn't know. I didn't think it'd be right to leave without saying so."

He shuts the door behind him as quietly as if we are still sleeping. Will rests his forehead against the back of my neck. I feel his breath and his kisses and for the physical sensation, I am grateful. This moment, I am warm. I am capable of feeling pleasure. The next moment, I sleep. It is another gift he has given me, unasked for, this ability to slip away into a deep, dreamless slumber.

We eat breakfast at 3 p.m. with the others. Tara insists she'll try black coffee like Will's.

I pour sugar into my cup. Sugar and more sugar. Let it cool so it tastes the way Jonah makes it for me. Tara reads the menu over Will's arm and says into his shoulder, "I'm hooking up with Hildie today if you're still around."

A sunbeam through the plate glass bakes my arm. Will's hand on my thigh gives me a little squeeze.

———

Will and I take the train back to his house. He unwraps a cookie he bought at the coffee shop in the station.

"I've never had one of these," I say. "Half-moon."

"Or a black and white," he says, tapping my forehead lightly. "Girl with her head in the clouds, clouds, clouds."

My appetite disappears for days, but today, I have it, first for breakfast, now for more than my half.

"I have no intention of seeing Hildie," he says. "I wish her well, but I don't have any feelings for her. Not anymore." This is less reassuring than he imagines it will be. The easy subtraction. "I don't know why Tara brought her up."

"Tara thinks I will be bothered by what bothers other people. Tara is a lucky girl."

"We don't have to see those people again," he says, and maybe he means it. "Whatever you want."

Whatever I want. Whatever I need. I wish we were home now, undressed, forgetful beneath his white sheets.

"Some days," I say, "I want to stand in one place and look around me. Then, as soon as I do, I want to move."

He could play guitar with the flat tips of his fingers, these fingers he uses to play with my fingers now. People would come to hear him, women especially. Women look at him when he walks by, when they step into our train car in search of a seat—this large-boned man with his long arms, his sharp-featured face that is most often set in a frown, though he can surprise you with a transformative smile that elicits response. This man has decided what we should have for dinner, has mapped subway routes and train schedules, has folded laundry and piled it, still warm from the dryer, into my lap. We won't stay like this forever. But this doesn't worry me. Instead, I worry that I'll never be able to predict my own reactions again. What will make me laugh? What will make me fling something against a wall? What will I covet? I worry that I will never again have one feeling uncomplicated by another equally as powerful.

Will must think if he chooses now to tell me he loves me, this will help. The train lurches out of the station, hurtles towards home.

We make love in the roommate's bed just for kicks. I ding the triangle and we're quiet until the ringing ebbs. Then, despite Will's weight on me, I close my eyes tight, leave us a while to the planets above, to just a few months before this when another night settled around me, where so many nights darkened towards day, but I cling to him, cling.

———

Cole writes me letters. I struggle with his handwriting, though it makes me happy to receive something in the mail, several pages long, full of comments on books he's reading, the view from the open door of an airplane. He describes himself as a boy—the home-done haircut that nicked his ear so bad it bled all the way to school, a dried thread of red along the luminous canals of his ear, his uniform's clip-on tie that he stuffed into his lunch box at the last bell, the way it smelled of cold cuts every morning when he put it back on.

I write back about my own life: walking barefoot over floor grates in our old house, my father's hacking cough, the sweaters I wore to school reeking of cigarettes. My mother's distracted parenting, packing a lunch without a sandwich in it, ironing all but one sleeve of a blouse. I was eight when my father died, heart attack on the kitchen floor. My mother used his insurance money to buy a women's fitness center and thus began her emancipation. A closet full of aerobic leotards in our new, antiseptic condo, a refrigerator filled with carrot sticks and yogurt. I knew so little about my father, I wrote. His smell, really. Drugstore aftershave. Wrigley's Spearmint gum in the pocket of his shirt. I remember his work pants stiff from cold on the clothesline. I have no idea who he was, only the useless adjectives my mother provides when I push her. How are we alike, he and I, I wonder? Does she see him in me in ways that surprise her?

I look for something that will keep Cole's letters safe and settle on an empty coffee can in the pantry, forget the letter though not its contents until Will discovers it one morning just as Jonas and Todd arrive with his parents. He's puzzled, smiles as if the surprise is for him. Then he says, "He writes to you? Why?"

"It's just something we do," I say. "It doesn't have anything to do with you."

Too late, I know how it sounds no matter what I meant.

Will balls the letter up as the front door opens. It takes him a minute to greet everyone. His mother insists on a tour of the place so he takes her. He says the house used to be a summer cottage, everything on Ways Beach was, but now they're mostly year-round, gutted like this one so from front yard to dining room, to deck, you see water. He sounds impatient with those copy-cat transformations though he loves the views, brings me to the windows for sunsets, storm clouds, striations of birds. His father yanks a suitcase from Jonas's grasp while Todd keeps a hand on the car trunk as if it needs bracing. He has a small bandage on his cheek where he's had a spot removed.

"I can lift the goddamned thing," the father says. What he means to say is, I don't need a fairy son to lift if for me.

Todd says, "Fingers, fingers," before he shuts the trunk and Jonas says to me under his breath, "I'll get the fucking cocktails."

In the morning, Will and I will drive the parents to a hotel in the city for a cousin's wedding, their mother excited about the Big Apple, their father damning hotel prices and noise pollution. The mother is small, round-faced like Jonas. Will has his father's face with and without the sneer, his father's body without the paunch.

"It's a great place, don't you think, Warren?" the mother says, breathy with clambering down stairs, peering through doorways, checking the views from every window.

"Sea makes things so damned damp," the father says.

After dinner, Jonas gets very silly on warm champagne he's dug out of the pantry and refused to share. Will is annoyed when he finds the empty bottle.

"This doesn't belong to me," he says.

"I used to save champagne," I say, partly to ease the tension, part-ly because I don't want to go back to the others sitting on the deck, the mother calling out the wrong names for constellations, the father chain-smoking to ward off mosquitoes, Todd fingering his incision and humming because he's no good at inspiring conversation even in the best of times.

"Oh, right, live for the present," Will says. "Drink someone else's champagne. Write secret letters to a man who is not your lover. Who might not be your lover. Stash things away in a space that wasn't yours to begin with."

Will's anger makes me stare at the tops of my bare feet. It makes me feel the same as everyone else.

"I won't use anything as an excuse," I say. "It's not fair."

Jonas laughs nervously. "Why, suddenly, am I plunged into total darkness?" he says. "Why do I feel I've just clicked through several channels and landed momentarily on a soap opera?"

Will drops the empty bottle into the recycling bin and it clinks against other bottles. He slams the closet door.

"If it helps, I will replace the champagne," Jonas says. "It's not worth an argument. I don't want you upset."

"She's fine," Will says. "Don't worry about her. Stop worrying about her."

"I just meant, why save anything you can buy at the store?" I say.

It is what I meant. Finding my way back to speaking aloud has been filled with challenges. Will admitted he watched me climb the steps to the upper deck of the ferry that first day and wondered if he could love someone who was so quiet. I have been called talkative. Approachable. Effusive. By people Will has never met.

Cole, the reader, the man who jumps out of planes, said the first time he met me, he was struck by my melancholy. A word Will would never use. He doesn't use words, really, except for directing people, for coaxing me during lovemaking, for passing along news. He might sign a card or send a postcard, but he would not write a letter. And I don't wish he would. I don't want him to be a composite of himself and anything or anyone else.

When their mother comes into the kitchen for a glass of water, I shut myself in the bathroom until I hear everyone go back outside.

Todd goes upstairs early. Will directs no comments in my direction, and Jonas gets so drunk he mutters Greek phrases under his breath that I'm sure must be disparaging. I go to bed, awakened an hour later by Jonas sitting beside me.

"No one dies from a little tiny mole, right?" he says.

"People die of every little thing," I say. "But Todd won't."

Jonas must be very drunk because he stretches out beside me and asks me to rub his back.

"How do you know he won't?" he asks.

"What if my boyfriend won a million dollars in the lottery? Wouldn't you think that your boyfriend's chances of winning were even slimmer now?"

"Your boyfriend is a big bully," he says.

Jonas and Todd don't get up to see us off. I'm sure Jonas eventually crawled into his own room with a headache and Todd would rather read an old *Newsweek* he found in the sofa cushions the night before than join us for breakfast. We drop the parents off in the hotel lobby. Will shows his mother where she can get a massage and a facial.

"Imagine that, Warren," she says. "I'd like to do that."

Then she is absorbed at the bank of elevators trying to discover which will take her to their floor. The father insists on lugging their bags, waves off bellhops.

Will decides to work for a few hours. We've spoken little this morning and it sinks a ball of worry in my gut that makes me aware that, sometimes now, I feel an old weightlessness. I have not had to work for his kindness, have come to him from a place where people granted me supreme forgiveness no matter what I did.

"Will," I say through the car window, as he drops me in front of the Metropolitan Museum. "You can read the letters, really. They're like conversations, just easier."

"I have to get to the office," he says, and presses the accelerator so I'll let go of the window. He really is a crazy driver.

"Please," I say. "There's lots of traffic. Take your time."

I consider not the odds in general, but only those pertaining to him.

Instead of trolling the galleries, I sit on the sculpture deck. I brought nothing to read and don't appreciate giant replicas of traffic cones and lug nuts, heavy objects anchored here. I think of hunting down watercolors, but I imagine the light inside, dimmed the way Will dims the lights every night for our dinner. The kind of light that cured my fear of darkness falling but that I have not entered into alone for months.

What does one do with a woman who moves in without asking and speaks very little? If you are Will, you grind coffee beans and take the sea canoe out for the afternoon. You read the newspaper or shop for dinner. You do all the things you've always done, but you keep an eye out. You bring her tea and suggest a walk along a rainy beach. You go to work and call from your desk a few times to pass along gossip about people she barely knows. You sit beside her and unbutton her shirt. You listen. Sometimes just for the sound of someone stepping out of the shower or closing a door. With your patience and your activity, you tether someone to daily life.

Though the city provides me no sense of direction, I look out over it, the trees always a surprise. It will never be my city, but I have loved its wild acceptance, the way it ignores me as I stare. It has made me feel ·I could get away with anything, that no one expects me to be whoever I used to be. No one expects me to be anything at all. I have had almost a year of it. The feeling that I both want something and don't want it. The understanding that any actions have such small consequences in a place as big as this.

It's why I slept with Cole just that once. Because never, in my settled life, my safe one, would I have considered it. Because I knew it could not change anything elemental. This is a world of secret-sharers. A noisy world full of unimaginable silence.

I had returned to the Berkshires house to pack. Jonas was teaching a class at a nearby college. Todd had gone sofa shopping alone. I liked thinking of him sitting back in movie-set living rooms, running his long fingers over the cushions, politely refusing the salesperson's help.

"If you'd like to see where I lived, come," I had written to Cole. "I won't stay long."

I didn't want to be there alone, though I needed to, the way I needed to roam through Ellis Island months before. My own clock. My own un-guided tour of the necessary spaces. But Cole would not ask questions. He already had the answers to questions other people hadn't asked me in years.

It happened almost as soon as he walked in. He had his coat on, a black wool jacket, damp from the rain. He smelled of being home at the end of a day, of ducking, at last, beneath a familiar frame and into your own yellow light. I remember his body beneath that coat, how surprisingly warm it was in comparison. We lay on the floor, boxes stacked around us as if we were in a block city, a child's creation. It was as wonderful as sex can be with someone you could love, but it was just an experience. Something I did on a rainy afternoon, something that will not happen again, something that inspired no guilt until Will discovered the letters. There are the feelings I have for Will and there are the feelings I have for other men. They must co-exist. It wasn't always so; I loved one person once, only that person; it isn't my choice that that love is mine still and must accompany all others.

Weight

I meet Will in the lobby of the apartment building. He's stopped for a haircut, no more parted on the side, boy's regular. Instead, his hair is shorter, combed off his face. He's so handsome this way I can't look at him. His hands search the mailbox for the key.

We sit beside each other on the twin bed. He tells me he didn't mean to be so angry about the champagne.

"Was it the champagne?" I say.

Quiet. Then he says, "I wish it was just the two of us."

I don't say it is, though I'm thinking it might as well be: On this bed, in this room. No matter that our minds are as crowded with people as the streets outside. Oh, the faces that pass us, familiar, fleeting. Come back, we say. Just so we are reminded of that gesture, the squint before you recognize me, the way your hair lifts off your forehead in a wind.

When we lie beside one another, we don't get up until it's dark and we're hungry.

"You haven't said anything about the haircut," he says. We're getting out of the shower, and he's rummaging for a comb in his travel case.

"I think you're beautiful," I say.

"And that's why you're so shy?"

"I'm a little overwhelmed by you, really. Your confidence. Your patience. You go about whatever it is you're doing as if that activity, that task, is the most absorbing thing."

"And you watch me."

"Like the day I met you. I stared and stared but I couldn't think what to say to you. I wondered if you'd stay with me, keep trying."

"So instead you stayed with me?"

I nod. Because I wanted to get here—to a place where I stand naked and, gently, he towels me off.

In the morning, picking up my clothes, I discover a vibrator under the bed. We get on our hands and knees and peer at it together. Many of his co-workers use the apartment but his boss had spent the previous week here after several nights of late meetings.

"I don't think that's his wife's," Will says.

He has this new man's haircut, but he's as thrilled as a boy. Then we laugh at ourselves on the floor like this and then we make love without a vibrator and it's something that doesn't make me wish for anything else.

Late to meet his parents, he holds my hand and we run through Central Park. It's misty and empty. A vendor rolls a cart past us. A horse stamps and sputters at the curb, its driver tightening harnesses with one hand, holding his coffee on the animal's back with another. Funny how you know as they are happening, the things you will remember.

At breakfast, Will's mother describes every hors d'oeuvre, includes details of each layer of the wedding cake.

Her son's ejaculate soaks the crotch of my underwear.

"Biggest waste of money I've ever seen," the father says. "My daughters got married in the back yard."

"Oh, Warren, you danced all night," the mother says, and he shrugs.

Will reads the paper and suggests we order bagels. His mother and I oblige. His father selects a Western, then waits outside and smokes.

I know his mother wants to talk, that our sitting here is taken as something more important than it is. She might be expected to tell me that Will nursed well and rolled over just at the right moment and smelled good out of his bath, but they grow up, these lovely, sweaty boys, and she is just another woman who will never know what a great lover her son is, his tenderness, his teasing. I have witnessed his desire, that moment he leaves earth, my arms and legs as tightly around him as if he was dying, and, I think, I have loved him anyway.

The mother says of the bride and groom, "I hope their love will last. Everything has changed so."

She doesn't speak to me, not really, not to Will, either, whose face is hidden behind the newspaper.

"It's true we don't love for the promise of long lives and progeny," I say. We love for something as immediate as the flush of anger or as debilitating as terror, but before I can say this, Will puts his paper down.

"And it's enough," I say. "To love that briefly, if that's what you get. It can be an archway, right? Not a whole corridor. Why pretend that just because something lasts in a way we can define it, it is love? Why is that its only test?"

Will's mother clears her throat, her hand fluttering at her shirt collar, her eyes round and magnified behind her glasses. I feel as I did the day before at the sculpture garden, looking down, unable to find a familiar spot below, a landmark that will allow me to say: I'm here and now I know where everything else must be. But I don't feel lost, just lighter, drifting, as bereft of resistance as I have ever been.

Will starts to rise, and I think he means to come to me.

But then the waiter sets down our breakfast, and Will sits. The father pulls open the door and heads for our table. Silverware clatters. From the kitchen we hear someone singing in Italian. Will does not look away from me and for a few seconds I stare back.

Then I bow my head and we eat in silence, absorbed by the plates before us, as gleaming white as bones that have never been forced to fuse together along a new line, a faint river, along the jagged fissure that even perfect healing leaves in its wake.

FINE CREATURES OF THE DEEP

Etta Ender's latest accusation was that our dog had dug up her phlox. Not just any phlox—thirty-year-old, purple-carpet-at-your-slippered-feet phlox, though it had passed by that fall into a frizzy, yellow creeper. She demanded I follow her into her yard, then pointed to the spot where phlox had flourished. A cherub atop a Roman column poured an empty urn into a ferociously dug hole.

When we let our dog, a nervous, nearly blind border collie, outside, she skulked close to the foundation, did her business, then whined at the back door. She spent her days beneath the kitchen table.

"Are you sure it was Winnie?" I said.

Etta glared at me, small eyes outlined in black, foundation blended seamlessly on her skin. She was sixty-something, but looked years younger, ready, though not quite old enough, for a *Modern Maturity* photo shoot. She had called me away from sliding boxes and a small plastic bathtub full of baby clothes across the seat of my car. Before my husband Andre got home, I would drop them off at Goodwill.

"Who else doesn't obey a leash law?" Etta squawked, hands on hips so narrow I wondered how she'd pushed three sons out between them, wondered how she had looked pregnant, though I doubted she would have been a belly-rubber. I doubted I would have been one, either, had my pregnancies worked out.

For the six weeks Andre and I had a baby in our home, Etta never ventured over to have a peek the way Regina Aulderson did or to offer up the plate of cookies and the homemade thumbless mittens Regina had, either. But those hips had delivered three children. She'd failed at none of it.

"What are you staring at?" Etta snapped.

Her husband Orin came around the corner of the garage, leaf blower roaring.

"Plenty of sunshine this week," he called over the racket. "No rain til Sunday!" Then he saluted triumphantly and disappeared again.

Etta huffed. "We expect the phlox to be replaced."

I had no idea where to begin looking for a plant that even I knew was out of season. Was there a greenhouse within a five-mile radius? I had lived here for three years and had no idea. Give me numbers that sprout in columns, that follow rules you have memorized, not things striving unpredictably towards the light. I'd spent planting seasons beneath fluorescent tubes, calculator keys more familiar to me than the faces of my loved ones until the foster care agency called and I left my barren cubicle to try motherhood.

"You've worked so hard to get where you are," my mother said when I told her I would stay home with a baby. "What makes you think raising a child will hold your interest? Especially someone else's child."

I told her the baby would start out as someone else's, yes, but . . .

"You've certainly read enough fairytales to believe in happy endings," she said. "You've just conveniently forgotten the roles of the stepmothers in them."

I never read fairytales.

"I'll replace the phlox," I said to Etta and hurried back to my car.

"Well, that's the easiest solution," Andre said when I told him.

"Except Winnie didn't do it."

"That's probably true." Andre was home after a day of mediation between the cafeteria workers' union and the trustees at a local university. On his way into the meeting, his suit had been splattered with ketchup from the protest and now it dried like thick blood on his lapel. "But there'll be no convincing her. Wait until she's off somewhere then leave the—what are they?—on her front steps."

If Etta had waited a day, I might have been as reasonable as Andre, but as I slid those baby things into the donation bin, the thought of Etta's small, perfectly manicured world made me retch into the weeds surrounding the parking lot. Now I stood in my kitchen about to cry over having to buy twenty dollars' worth of flowers to keep a crazy woman quiet.

"She doesn't like me," I said. From her spot under the table, Winnie whimpered. "It's just like the bird bath. She didn't come and crick her finger at you. She waited until she saw me, then she marched over insisting we breed mosquitoes to torture her. The wood pile, too. I was the one who had to walk the property line with her so I could see how four inches of our logs had trespassed."

I tried muting my sniffles, but Andre hugged me, resting his chin on the top of my head. He smelled of tomatoes and salt. "I helped you move those logs, right? And I told her we chose to leave the bird bath. I didn't abandon you to the nutty woman's clutches."

His voice was soft, but I didn't know if it was for my benefit or for Winnie's since she peed when startled.

"It's hard to put yourself out there, Polly. To reach out, especially after what's happened to us, but you are doing the big thing. Let the truth satisfy you."

Not a baby, not the peaceful coexistence of neighbors, just the truth.

That became a lot easier as soon as Etta stopped speaking to us. In the grocery store, she sniffed mushrooms and ignored me as I maneuvered my cart next to hers and grabbed an avocado. Out for her daily exercise, she found Regina Aulderson's chimney endlessly absorbing if I happened to be outside, too, checking my mailbox.

Andre said it was my imagination. "It's not possible that someone just stops speaking. An adult. Just speak first. You'll see."

He tried a few days later as Etta and Orin walked to their car, Etta in a pink silk pantsuit and straw hat though it was cloudy. Orin had stopped calling extended weather forecasts through the naked forsythia to me when Etta was in earshot, but waved energetically when she wasn't watching. Now, he swung suitcases into their trunk.

"You moving away on us?" Andre called. He had just returned from walking Winnie who wound her leash between his legs, cowering.

Orin, who always had a Band-Aid on one knuckle or another, said, "Running off to join the circus."

"You won't be such a comedian if we miss the plane," Etta said, over the hood of the car, and climbed in.

"Morning, Etta," Andre said.

She slammed the door, glared at the garage door as Orin backed them out.

Two days later, their son's truck sat in their driveway. The next morning, it hadn't moved. No lights glowed in the house and though the screen door was closed, the front door stayed ajar. I wondered later whether we shouldn't have called someone—but who? We had no numbers for Etta's sons, burly men whose beards and bellies made them look alike from a distance. One had children though we never saw them in the Enders' pool. Lobstermen all, the sons removed their boots before stepping into Etta's house. I'd seen them on the welcome mat Christmas day.

At my mailbox, the wind tore an envelope out of my hand. It fluttered about, broken-winged thing, and settled on Regina Aulderson's walk. The deadbolt thunked in the front door and Regina opened it.

"Polly?" she said. "Is anything wrong?"

"Oh no," I said. "The wind took a piece of mail."

Regina leaned out her doorway, television inside tuned to *As the World Turns*. A couple kissed open-mouthed in a hospital.

"Enders are gone on a real adventure, aren't they?" she said. "I bet it's a long way down to those islands. Orin aims to swim with turtles."

So the Enders hadn't run off to join the circus. They'd left for Barbados where, we heard much later, Orin did swim with giant turtles. Etta had sat beneath an umbrella at the pool as she does all summer at home, Etta who looked a bit like a turtle, neck skin taut, eyes wide-spaced, nose tented between her cheek bones. The year before, when she'd let her dark hair turn gray, I'd thought her more badger, but recently her reptilian visage had returned.

"Their son Donald says they're enjoying it," Regina said. "He's a good kid, that Donald, checks up on things when they're away." She nodded towards the truck.

"They could have asked me," I said. "I'm home all day."

"So you are now? Home?"

I thought of telling Regina that my colleagues had saved my desk hoping for the return of the person who put the coffee on every morning and turned the lights out every night. The custodians must have missed me most of all. But if I let Regina know how indispensable I was, I'd also have to explain how I would never go back to a place that had chipped in to buy me a baby stroller. I shut my eyes. If Regina noticed, she said nothing.

"The truck's been there," I said.

"He must have taken their car to drop them at the airport. Don't know if I'd be brave enough to drive it around after that, though. Etta keeps it just so, but they must've worked something out. How we do get talked into things. You know how it is with mothers and their kids."

Then she stopped and blinked at me, a woman who had a baby one day and a few months later did not.

"Oh, dear, you know what I mean," she said. "M-m-maybe it's the same with your mom."

My mother? No. For every favor I requested, my mother had a facial or a heat treatment or a facial and a heat treatment before her luncheon with Father Lulio. Or she required resting up from one of the above. If I could have depended on her, who knows how the placement might have worked out? Instead, baby Henry fussed until he wailed, wailed until he vomited, and vomited until he'd emptied his stomach. How does one quiet an unhappy baby, a daughter might have asked a mother? Regina maybe. Regina would have known. But the only thing I came up with was running water in the sink. This pacified him long enough for me to feed him, but when I turned the water off, he started again.

The social worker advised us to try foster care with an older child next time.

"This baby," the social worker had said to us, "might have colic. That would be a hard thing for first time caretakers to adjust to."

Henry jerked his arms and legs in his seat at her feet, his tiny face red.

"He's a good sleeper," Andre offered, since by the time he got home every night, the baby slept soundly, exhausted by a day of screeching.

"I'm sorry." The social worker's hair hung in a thick braid down her back. Veins roped through her long hands as she fiddled with the folder on her lap. "We did inform you of the trial period. We must be certain that the child can thrive in his new home."

She's taking him, I thought. And for a minute I considered she'd fix him and bring him back, like a small appliance.

"Has it ever happened before," Andre asked, "that a placement didn't work out this quickly?"

The social worker clucked at the baby and spoke to him when she said, sweetly, "Oh, we'll work out a placement all right."

When she drove off with Henry, Andre had said to the window: "You could have said something."

I thought about Henry, the experiment in his tiny, weight-losing form, his wrinkled feet drawing back from the toes of his terrycloth suits until the doctor followed the nurse into the examining room and studied the numbers on the scale.

Andre had turned and scanned the room full of baby things: seats and blankets, a few toys the baby never glanced at though I'd shaken them furiously in his face. "We'll put this stuff away for next time," he said, carefully packing the boxes I had loaded into the car the day Etta confronted me about the phlox.

At least that time when we lost a baby, there was no blood.

When our water bill arrived, Andre spent a Saturday with a drop-light in the basement searching for leaks. He finally came to bed with a cobweb in his hair, and I told him babies used lots of water. He lay still as I unfolded the mysteries of rewarming bathwater and presoaking laundry, of boiling bottles, and scrubbing surfaces several times a day.

"So you did try," he said. "How could I not have seen how much work this was?"

Long after I thought he'd fallen asleep, he said, "I feel better about the water now. I'd had an idea the walls might cave in with some mysterious leak. It's good to know it was just the baby."

On Regina's step, I opened my eyes. In Etta's driveway, the truck sat, a faded gray with a ruffle of rust along its underside.

"The Enders took Etta's car to the airport," I said. "Donald didn't drive them."

"Oh, my," Regina said. "Do you suppose anything's wrong?"

As she tapped her lip, I examined my house: standard New England

Cape Cod, beige, green shutters. Copper-colored leaves covered grass that had needed one last mowing. We'd removed the window boxes when we moved in and now darker beige rectangles marked their absence. The dry bowl of the bird bath held more leaves, a slick of dark water atop them. We had bought the house because it had a yard and three bedrooms.

The Enders studded their shrubbery with purple cabbages and rust-colored mums. A basket of gourds sat propped against their lamp-post on a bed of straw. They'd left everything the way things should be left: immaculate, just in case you aren't coming back. That way, your sisters-in-law don't discover the closets you jam things into before they come. They don't empty out your underwear drawer, noting the stained crotches of your panties and forgetting what you looked like gussied up for a black tie wedding.

"The door's open, too. But I'm sure it's nothing," I said. Nights, the temperature had begun to drop so much, our radiators clicked on. "Then again, sad things happen, even to good people."

Which, you might conclude, was a curse that backfired. And that didn't.

Though we were not the childless couple whose dog becomes their child, when we woke up the next morning and found Winnie's stiff body beneath the table, we both cried. We'd barely looked at Winnie when we'd had Henry, but after he left, I appreciated that she ate quickly, kept everything down, and slept most of the day.

"We aren't cut out for this," Andre said. "This taking care. This cultivating."

"Yes you are," I said. "You never yelled when she peed in the house. You gave her Benadryl before thunderstorms."

He squatted beside her, smoothed the long hair of her ears, wiped his nose on the cuff of his shirt. "Thanks for saying that, Polly," he said.

I waited to hear how he would reassure me, but he remained over her body. He's hurting, too, I thought. He does love you, he said he always would, he promised. I chanted this silently until I felt a little dizzy and then I held onto the edge of the counter.

He said, "It's been such a difficult time. Between the baby, the dog, and this silly stuff with you and the neighbors . . . I never know what to expect when I walk in the door."

Suddenly, I hated the way his shoulders rounded—had always rounded—beneath the cotton blend of his shirt, and, though I guessed that it was scientifically impossible, I said, "Let's see how silly you think I'm being now that Etta Enders poisoned your dog."

He stood slowly and took his glasses off to rub his eyes. Then he turned and stared blindly behind me through the window at the Enders' house.

"Oh my god," he said, and I felt triumphant. Why shouldn't he believe her capable of that? But then, he hurried to put his glasses back on and said, "There's a police car in their driveway."

Though he was, I am certain, convinced for one glorious second, that his wife wasn't so crazy after all.

Etta had hounded her son for years to remove the half-wall that divided her kitchen and dining area. As a surprise, he had planned on her coming home to the finished project. Unfortunately, he hadn't gotten far with the demolition before his heart stopped. A fluke. A one-in-a-million freak of physiology. It took the captain of his lobster boat and Regina calling on the same day before the police found him on the highly polished floor of Etta's kitchen, a shattered cookie jar (empty) and a shelf of unsoiled cookbooks scattered about him. Hours later, the clueless parents stepped off the plane, well-rested, intimate with turtles.

When Andre pulled into the driveway the next night, his headlights blinded me as I carried a pot of soup. I drew up to his closed window and looked in.

"For the Enders," I said, steam rising from beneath the lid.

Andre's hair was always a bit greasy despite his daily shower, his glasses smudged with fingerprints.

"I can't go over with this," he said, lifting his scarred briefcase off the seat. "But this is a nice thing to do, Polly. This is the right thing."

Andre might not admit it, but until he put aside his suspicions about Winnie, he would be hesitant to reach out despite the tragedy. He had buried Winnie in our back yard the night before, digging the hole with the help of a headlamp we kept with the camping supplies we hadn't touched in years. I did feel big about offering this gift to the Enders. Despite my shortcomings, here I was: the one making the thoughtful gesture. I didn't have to be reminded not to slouch as I knocked.

Regina cracked open their door, poked her head out.

"I won't come in," I said. "I just wanted to bring this."

"Polly," she said, the way a mother might say your name looking up from the card you've made her. "This is so sweet."

If she didn't have the soup in her hands she would have hugged me. This made me teary. I hadn't intended to feel grateful to Regina, her chest flattened beneath motley layers of long-sleeved shirts and topped with a sweater vest. A breeze tossed limbs on the ancient pines along our border, the shushing of their branches a soft percussion.

Regina leaned forward. "My dear," she whispered, eyes welling, "of course you would understand this mother's pain."

And I admit it, I felt hopeful. Felt that what I wanted—and it surprised me as well—was for Etta to like me. Etta and everyone else. It mattered that now, at last, even Etta might see what a deserving person she had tormented. Relief surged through me. Then a hot current of pity and forgiveness until Etta crossed the entryway without glancing my way. She'd applied makeup. A belted black cardigan hung to her knees. She wore somber, square heels. A thick gold hoop in her ear caught the light and flashed at me.

Regina opened her mouth as if to say something. *Look at the lovely soup Polly's brought,* perhaps, but when Etta strode forward, Regina turned back to me, embarrassed. When she slid the door closed, I stared at the Indian corn tacked onto it.

"She's in shock," Andre said, when I told him. "She thought you were the press."

"If I stand here long enough, will you list every possible excuse? Her grief has blinded her? She's heavily medicated? She thought Regina was talking to herself?"

"She might be medicated."

"It would help to hear you say I'm not a terrible person. That I'm not a person who is so totally unlovable that even my good deeds get me shunned."

"Shunned? Who shuns you? She lost her son. Do you think she can keep track of your petty feuding when she's in so much pain? Don't go looking for trouble, Polly. It's going to take all the strength that woman can summon to get her through this."

"Oh, it hurts to lose a son, does it?" I said and watched the look of confusion pass over my husband's face.

Orin returned my empty pot with a note attached: *Dear Polly and Andre, Thank you for your delicious soup. It has been the only thing I've been able to eat. Polly has not been very considerate of us in the past, but perhaps this is a sign she can be a good neighbor after all. Though now, of course, we understand none of that really matters. Sincerely, Etta.*

Andre shrugged. I put the card on the windowsill over the kitchen sink, same place I had displayed the congratulations cards when Henry had come home.

The next morning, sky still pink, the sound of Orin's leaf blower woke me. He blasted his driveway clean, the sidewalk, the street. Andre groaned and padded into the bathroom. I went downstairs and turned the heat up under the soup pot. By the time Andre walked into the kitchen, fresh spinach steamed in broth.

"Dinner?" he said.

"Soup for Etta."

Reverend Bob answered the door this time, or rather he opened it on his way out and discovered me trying to knock without spilling the contents.

"So kind of you," he said. Behind him, the Enders bumped one another trying to see who he spoke to.

"If soup is all you can eat," I said, "then it's the least I can do."

I pushed the pot around him and then past Orin, the Band-Aid today stuck on his left thumb, and towards the pale hands, gold rings as big as arthritic knuckles, of Etta, who drew back.

I felt a kiss on my cheek and assumed Reverend Bob's humanity had gotten the better of him. My mother had been sleeping with a priest for years. A peck from a Methodist didn't alarm me. But Orin had kissed me as he lifted my offering and because he had an awkward angle, most likely burned his hands doing it.

"We can't begin to thank you," he said, so close to my face, I noticed a freckle overlapping the rim of his lower eyelid.

When I looked up, Etta had vanished.

The pot appeared on the doorstep a few days later, this time with a generic thank you from the funeral director. Etta resumed her morning walks, rhinestones glinting on the edges of her enormous sunglasses, lipliner, lipstick, artful. Routines, as therapists will tell you, help the world return in palatable bites. When I raised my hand from where I stood in the driveway, she ignored me. When I deliberately met her on her return route, she put her head down, plowed past.

I called Andre at work. "Because my dog dug up her flowers?"

He said, "Maybe it's because you didn't replace them."

"And this is still important to her?"

"She doesn't need a rational excuse, Polly. She only needs a target for her anger."

When I tried to find the phlox and failed, I made another pot of soup. Why not? I'd received notice to return to work the following week if I wanted my job. The patience of colleagues is fleeting. But the compassion of neighbors? Let's pretend, I thought, that it has no bounds.

I waited until Etta's car drove in then approached their house. Orin vacuumed pine needles from the border. When he saw me, he paused and touched the rim of his baseball cap. Etta opened the car door nearly knocking into me and gasped.

"Mushroom barley," I said. She wore leather gloves the color of butterscotch and by all appearances, just as smooth. She had no choice but to accept the gift I offered her and to sit back down, the pot on her lap.

Orin stared at me until Etta's voice roused him, then he tried hurrying towards her to help but stumbled as the vacuum sucked in the cuff of his pants.

———

So went fall. Despite my vow never to return, Andre insisted I resume work. I buried my face in tax forms, clacked away on my calculator as if I was sending messages worldwide via Morse code. Each time I returned home and found the empty pot on my step, I stayed up late to fill it: chicken noodle with tiny meatballs, cream of tomato, carrot and dill. As the contents simmered on the stove, I set out for the all-night grocery store to buy the next day's ingredients at a time when I'd encounter no mothers stuffing babies with cheese slices and animal crackers, when I'd notice no fat legs kicking happily in carriage seats.

Regina asked for recipes and spread word up and down the street about my generosity. She knocked on my door one afternoon as I hung up my coat.

"You know, Polly, everyone surrounds you those first few days of your loss, but only rare friends remember how long healing takes."

She handed me a brown paper bag with an afghan that one of

her sisters had knit, a blanket done in yellow and mint green yarn in a raised pattern that looked like shells. The kind of gift old aunties bring to baby showers. The attached note said: A little something for a woman who does so much.

I leaned against the doorframe and lifted the blanket to my nose expecting baby, but it gave off a slightly plastic smell.

"Lovely," I said, and Regina wrung her hands and walked away.

Andre peered into the bag and retrieved the note as I made dinner. "What's going on?" he asked.

"My kind deeds are earning me a reputation."

"Your kind deeds are getting obsessive. What is it that you seek?"

I peered into his face, my breath steaming his glasses. "Oh, Wiseman," I said. "I seek to be recognized as a good person, to cook up my sanity up pot by pot and bring it to a crazy woman who refuses to say one face-to-face thank-you."

"She is a grieving woman," Andre said, moving away from me. "A grieving mother."

"But what would I know about that, is that what you're saying?"

"You would know everything about that. That's what I'm saying."

I drew a hot bath for myself and climbed into the tub as the water ran, drowning out Andre's movements downstairs, the wind outside. I had wished, of all things, to bathe with my baby, to slip naked into warm water with his dimpled body in the morning when sun lit the bathroom, fell upon the water in a wide beam, his cooing amplified, my hands soaping his back, steam forming curls at the base of his neck. But Henry had not been fat, had loved his bath only when the water ran. When I turned the faucet off, his bottom lip protruded, his eyes widened and his terror reverberated off the tiles.

I stayed away from the Enders, but a few weeks before the holidays, Orin had finished the chores in his own yard and started on ours. He chopped up a dead tree and sent it through his log splitter, stacked our woodpile as if it would form the wall of a real house. He skimmed leaves out of our gutters, nailed a shutter that had been banging about since we moved in. The first snowfall, I returned home from the dentist to Orin snowblowing our driveway. When I stepped out of my car, he trotted over to sprinkle rock salt in my path. One side of my mouth still felt the effects of Novocain.

"You don't have to do all this," I slurred.

"Well, you really fixed me up with all that soup," Orin said. "Only thing I ate for weeks."

"I thought I was overdoing it," I said. "I thought it might remind you both too much."

He shook his head and smiled, and either he blushed or the cold reddened his cheeks.

"Funny thing is, we never forget so there's no such thing as being reminded."

I studied the neatly carved path at my feet, thought of red sleds, snow boots, wet clothes that would never be strewn in my entryway after a day of making snow forts.

"Mind if I distract myself a little?" he said. "There's lots to take care of here."

I shook my head, held my hand over the numbness, wished for two full body doses of such a miracle drug—one for me, one for my yard boy. Instead, I dug a snow shovel out of the garage and cleaned off the steps. I swept snow off the lids of the garbage cans, the hood of my car. I followed Orin to Regina's where we dug out her mailbox and scraped the ice off her car windows.

When we finished, he patted my arm through my heavy coat.

"See what I mean?" he said. "Almost time to go to bed and almost tired enough to sleep."

But all I felt was a desperate need to keep going.

"I'll put a pot of curried squash on," I said. "Pick it up in a hour or so."

Andre said nothing when Orin knocked on the door.

"I've missed Polly's soup," he said.

Andre clapped him on the shoulder. He watched him walk down our driveway and up his own. I went upstairs hoping to avoid discussion, but Andre found me in the bathroom contemplating my hair in the mirror. Lusterless with streaks of gray, it resisted my efforts to tie it back or to smooth it away from my face. Now Andre stroked it.

"I'm worried about you, Polly," he said. "I'm going to cancel this trip."

His carry-on sat in the hallway, packed for a weekend conference in New York.

"I'm fine, really. I had a good day," I said. "Orin is teaching me the power of distraction. We shoveled snow. That's why I made the soup. You can see he appreciates it."

I hated the olive tones of my skin, the circles under my dark eyes, the way my face gave away my age now. Too old, it said. Dried up on the outside, too.

"Still, I think I'd better stay home."

"And baby-sit. Because you told me not to make soup and you were right. I was making it for the wrong reasons. All this time, I did it out of anger. But as it turns out, I was doing good. Why should Orin suffer because his wife is so cold? I'm going to make soup, Andre. Maybe not as often, but I'm not stopping just because that nut thinks I'm being spiteful."

"My love," Andre said. "It's time to call Millicent."

"And tell her what? That I'm being too thoughtful? Oh, wait, even better. I'll call her and say I used to moan about wanting a baby and then I got one and didn't know what to do with it so now my every act is scrutinized for underlying proof of my instability."

"We lost a child," he said. "Why wouldn't we need help with that?"

"Millicent winters in Mexico."

"Therapists don't leave for entire seasons."

"She's very good at what she does. She doesn't foster dependencies."

He let his hand drop down my back and stood for a moment when I should have turned and held him. Then he walked out. A man who had considered himself a father.

I went downstairs and cut my hair very short using scissors from the knife block. By the time I got to bed, Andre slept.

Rain that Saturday kept me indoors boiling chicken carcasses for broth. I liked the sound of the rain, especially car tires through puddles. So this is what the baby heard, I thought. This slow motion, glass shattering music. I emptied closets, tossing almost new clothes into garbage bags and dragging them to the curb, washed walls, bed-spreads, curtains.

After I removed all of our pictures from the walls and dusted the backs of them, I dumped a bag of vegetables into broth. I had an idea of making peace by speaking for it, explaining myself to Etta. Why rely on symbolism, on actions? Maybe all this time, she just hadn't understood my intentions.

The rain had stopped but the temperature had dropped, coating every surface with ice. I expected to see Orin out with his pick and rock salt, wished for him since I slipped several times. Broth burned my hands through my gloves, soaked the cuffs of my jacket. Navigating the slight slope of their driveway proved impossible so instead I found clumps of grass poking out from the sheen and leapfrogged across their yard.

Etta appeared behind the storm door in a red silk robe and black mules. I noticed a coffee-colored stain down the front of the robe and then that one of the pockets was torn at the corner and stuffed with tissues. She wore no make-up. I wondered if I'd woken her though it was afternoon, but the television played and something else—a radio closer to the front door.

"What do you want?" she said.

"I wanted to give you this."

Her face contorted, her blue eyes bulging, her neck taut. "Keep your fucking soup." Spittle hit the glass.

"Etta," I said. "Please. Orin will eat this. It's the only thing I myself can eat since—"

"Orin is delirious with fever," she said through the glass. "He insists you're going to run away together."

She slammed the door. The lock turned. I set down the pot and stepped away.

"I lost my son." Etta's muffled voice rose. "I lost my son."

In my kitchen, I hung my coat over a chair. I'm done, I thought. Every day, Etta Enders, dolled up in the gold jewelry she'd bought on their last cruise, made up like a perfume saleswoman at the mall, encountered people who had no idea what hell she lived in. Every day, I passed women whose suffering I could not imagine, poised as I was over bus schedules or the fine print on legal documents for estate planning, trying to decipher restaurant menus, fighting back my own images of those first few tiny t-shirts in my laundry basket, the bald dome of Henry's sleeping head in the center of my bed. Why had I considered it lucky that at last someone might know what I felt?

I heard banging and moved to the window. Outside Etta beat the ice with a metal shovel. She wore Orin's orange parka over her bathrobe and hadn't changed out of her mules. Ice chips flew about her head like failed pyrotechnics. She chiseled a jagged path towards my bird bath, tossed aside her shovel and grabbed the glossed-over bowl with bare hands, grunting as she tugged. The ice had cemented the bird bath in place. When she tried to straighten, her hands stuck. There she stood, hunched over and howling.

It never occurred to me to save her. I thought it melodramatic to call 911 and useless to call Orin. Regina hobbled out to the end of her driveway.

"What's happened?" she cried. "Etta? Etta!?"

But Etta's bawling drowned her out and when Regina tried crossing to her, she fell, banging her head against the shellacked curb and losing consciousness, her hand tipping out into the street.

"Now that's an emergency," I said and dialed the police station.

When both ambulances pulled away—one with Regina's groggy self strapped to a gurney and one with Etta sitting up inside it, fat bandages around her hands—the officer knocked on our door.

"I made her soup after her son died," I said. "And she tried to steal my bird bath."

He wrote it all down as earnestly as if I'd witnessed murder.

"Did you offer her any assistance once you realized she was stuck?" he asked. Though young, he might have been bald beneath his cap. He was too handsome in his uniform to consider one of those hats with the earmuffs attached so now his ears reddened with cold.

"I've also just lost a child," I said.

He stopped writing and looked up at me, his blue eyes wide.

"I am sorry, ma'am," he said. "I had no idea."

"You wouldn't," I said. "You wouldn't have any idea."

When I entered Orin's dark room and put my hand on his burning forehead, he whimpered.

"You're going to be okay," I said. "I can take care of you."

He nodded as if he believed me.

I drew him a cool bath, stared out at the street where the officer sat in his car and wrote his report. His lights flashed against the glittery world, pulsing, silvery blue heartbeats. On mantles, in hallways, on polished tables in the corners of rooms, clocks ticked in Etta's home. A candle burned on the vanity. Pink flowered towels hung from their racks as if no one had considered wiping a hand with them. The water ran and ran, filling the gleaming tub. From far away, I heard

Orin's voice call my name, but not as if he needed something, just as if he wanted to remind himself that I'd come.

"I'm here," I said. "I'm here." I repeated it and repeated it until the words made no sense beyond the sounds of their syllables.

Steam fogged the mirror where Etta studied herself every day before greeting only some parts the world. I trawled my hand through the water and imagined myself somewhere else, clinging to turtle backs, perhaps, floating through the fairy hair of seaweed. I imagined fat babies slipping out from between my legs and spiraling through bubbles, laughing babies, buoyant mother—all of us determined never to return, but to stay here in this world of muted sounds, communing joyfully with fine creatures of the deep.

END OF STORY

Colin had left Maureen once she confessed the affair. He wished she hadn't confessed; he had suspected nothing. Even if he had, he would not have had courage to confront her, would have gone on in their marriage the way, he assumed, people went on. Not happy, but committed. Commitment he understood. You said something and you meant it. Besides, if he had suspected her, he would have thought: These things don't happen in my life, in the lives of people I know. In his siblings' lives, for example. All eight of them were married to good people though Kathleen's husband drank too much. But there was Colin—always-quick-with-a-witty-comeback Colin, without-a-care-in-the-world Colin, a man who had trouble getting people to take him seriously—with his wife sitting on the edge of his bed in the middle of the night and waking him: I want to tell you something. I haven't been faithful.

Though he couldn't have thought so at the time, that was the easier revelation to bear. Curiosity fled. He couldn't imagine it mattering with whom she slept. But Maureen had suddenly gotten very attached to whole truths. Kevin. She said the name before Colin had time to turn on the light.

"Kevin?" It took him a minute to picture the young man he'd hired to run the youth programs at the Y. The kid, the *kid,* who'd arrived for his interview twenty minutes late without an apology. Who shook his head to clear dark bangs off his forehead. Who convinced Colin's daughter Megan to let go of Maureen's leg the first day of camp by pulling out a scooter board and dragging it around the gym until she hopped on.

"But I'm a nice guy," Colin had said. He repeated it as he packed a few things into a gym bag. Because now he had to leave. This is why people leave, he remembers thinking. This is the kind of feeling that drives them into a life they never imagined for themselves.

— ▬ —

Two years later, Colin watched Rosanna, his girlfriend—ridiculous to have to call someone that after all these years, but there he was— spill coffee on the floor.

When she glanced around for something to wipe it up with, Colin said, "Don't use the sponge. You shouldn't use something on the floor that you'd use for dishes."

He would not have had to tell Maureen this. Did he say that out loud?

Rosanna ripped a paper towel off the roll and wiped furiously. "I know you think I'm an idiot," she said. "I must be, right, if I'm so happy with you, I'm not looking for some young thing to screw around with?"

Colin winced at the assault, but that was Rosanna, emotional to the point of thoughtlessness. He had told Rosanna so little about his life. It was hard to say Maureen's name, harder to say his daughter, Megan's, but, of course, he had told Rosanna why the marriage had ended. He told her Maureen had cheated and he told her with whom.

"And I left," he had said, shrugging.

This was months ago. Rosanna, who had been sitting on the couch sideways, legs curled up beneath her as she listened, said, "You felt you had no other choice."

Which was exactly how he had felt, how he felt still.

Now, Colin was finally getting some life back. Not his life. That life still felt like the one he had had with Maureen and their daughter, but now he had a girlfriend and people knew it. Well, most people.

Rosanna tossed the soiled paper towels in the trash. "I'm never going to be what you want," she said. "Especially if you keep wanting what you had."

Colin hadn't expected this. It took him a second to say, "I'm awfully glad you're not Maureen." Closer to the truth was that he didn't want her to be *that* Maureen, the Maureen whose infidelity had nearly destroyed him.

The Maureen who, two days ago, had asked him to move back in, to try again. Although Rosanna, of course, knew nothing of this.

Even so, she looked as though she might cry. She was young enough to cry. Twenty-six to Colin's thirty-three, which felt, which looked—he had gone completely gray, slept poorly—like fifty-three. Rosanna had large eyes, brown, thick-lashed, that made her look sweet. She pushed her dark hair, chin-length, back with a cloth headband. She had a square face, a small nose at its center like a beak. He wouldn't have considered her a magazine beauty, but there was something arresting in her face, something that made men turn to watch her when she and Colin walked into a restaurant, something that made him want to take her places even though he couldn't afford to. Even Maureen's extraordinary blue eyes couldn't make her anything more than plain.

"What have I ever done to make you think I'm stupid?" Rosanna said.

Fall in love with me, he thought, but he said, "Of course I don't think you're stupid. I don't know why I say what I say. I don't know why I don't trust you to do the right thing."

"Oh, Colin, we both know the answer to that."

When they were teenagers, a topic of conversation between Colin and Maureen had been: Do you trust me? Can I trust you? As if they were giving it away in one lump sum. As if they could never give these things—body parts, secrets—to anyone else again. He had trusted her and his recognition of this had stunned him, had made him so happy, he let out his barking laugh for days afterwards though he might be in the middle of a chemistry experiment or setting the table for dinner, his sisters looking at him as if he was choking on something and deserved to die for his carelessness.

Years later, when he and Maureen learned their second baby would be born with complications, a brain stem, but no brain (a stalk of cauliflower, Colin imagined, with its floret snapped off) he thought about those first discussions with Maureen. They didn't talk like that anymore. He couldn't imagine anyone talking that way once they grew up, had children. More than the sex, those revelations (Hers: My parents sleep in separate rooms though they pretend otherwise, I stole money from a gym locker in ninth grade, I believe in reincarnation; His: My father can not fall asleep unless my mother is asleep first, I bit Nora Fallon on her cheek in first grade because I wanted to see if it was as soft as it looked, I find confession cathartic) thrilled him.

But the discussions about the baby were different. In bed at night, both he and Maureen stared at the ceiling, Colin afraid to touch her and Maureen aware of it. They had gone to Mass together for years, St. Michael's, the parish they'd grown up in. They would have the baby. They didn't listen closely to any other options, nor did they weigh them lying together in the dark. When the baby was born, Maureen had named him Michael after that parish, had held him in her arms after he died. Colin hadn't expected him to have a head, he realized. His thoughts had gone so crazy. Michael had a face, impossibly small since he was born seven weeks early. Michael. It was like throwing away a perfectly good name, but they needed something on his tombstone.

After Michael's death, Maureen watched their daughter Megan who was learning to climb stairs and open cupboards. Maureen's vigilance distracted her, her body, young then and used to rigors—she had been a distance runner, a good one, in college—healed. It was as if one hard layer had sloughed off and beneath it, a softer Maureen, a Maureen more inclined to sigh, to lie in bed naked with their daughter who sucked a sippy cup. With Colin, even, she used a quieter voice, demanded nothing.

Colin grew quiet, assumed the demeanor of a deep thinker irrevocably scarred. A person he had never imagined himself becoming. He felt deserving of people's compassion, even his wife's. When he returned to work after his bereavement leave, people's laughter startled him. The correspondence piled on his desk, the ringing telephones, the demands for new flotation devices, renewed membership forms, less chlorine in the pool, paralyzed him, but it was the general impatience of the world, the headlong rush to the next thing, that left him sitting in his office with the lights off after everyone else had gone home.

Maureen had tried to talk to him, but he uttered one-word answers or responded with silence. When she asked him finally, to make love to her, he struggled to do it, he who had followed this woman around since he entered eighth grade at the parish school and discovered her sitting one seat ahead of him in homeroom.

"It's as if you blame me," she said, when they had finished and lay quietly on their own sides of the bed.

He didn't, but what he didn't explain was how different she felt to him now that her body had carried that poor child.

During those first weeks of grief, he had not asked himself if he still loved her. Marriage wasn't only about love, not, at least, love for one another. He needed to be alone, he realized, a man who had never been alone, who had moved from a house with nine children to his first home with his wife. He had not considered that Maureen might not have wanted such isolation. He fully intended to return to her when this grief subsided. I'll be back, he might have told her. Trust me. But neither of them ever talked about trust any more.

In the tiny kitchen of the apartment she rented, Rosanna packed for a picnic. Colin felt foolish having never been on one and foolish for going now. These forced romantic encounters, he imagined, ended in mosquito bites and sudden changes in the weather. And now because of the spilled coffee comment, her heart had clearly gone out of it, too. She slammed the refrigerator shut, shoved a wedge of cheese into the cooler, and plunked down on the lid to secure it.

"You don't have to help," she said. "I know it's not your idea. It's a silly idea. An idea concocted by a woman who used to think highly of herself but who has suddenly succumbed to staging romantic interludes."

He laughed the old Colin laugh, a loud eruption of something familiar. Something from his first life. He loved the way Rosanna could force that out of him, could resurrect a rare, painless part of his old life. The brooding, wounded, nice guy, victim thing he clung to in most settings scared Rosanna, he suspected, but he couldn't let go. Except for these brief, glorious outbursts. I can't go back to that house, he thought, remembering Maureen on the steps the morning she had asked him back, the door opened a crack behind her, over her shoulder, the yellow light of the kitchen at the end of the hall. Why would I go back?

"Cheer up," he said, pulling Rosanna up and wrapping his arms around her. She didn't hug him back but folded in half. He wouldn't remind her not to round her shoulders. "Maybe it will rain. Besides, I thought we'd stop at my mother's on our way out."

She straightened, stared at him.

"I'm meeting your mother?" She exaggerated her surprise. "But it's only been six months. Next thing you know, you'll be introducing me to your kid."

Colin squinted as if she'd just switched on a light in a comfortably dark space.

In a neighborhood whose houses peeled more and more each time he drove by them, the gray shingles of his mother's house maintained their dignity. The metal porch swing was empty, lace curtains covered the front windows, geraniums bloomed dutifully in flower boxes Colin and his brothers had built one summer instead of going to camp like the O'Driscolls and the Callaghys. How had this house ever gotten so quiet? So many inevitabilities had eluded him, it seemed. So many endings he had no imagination to predict.

His mother sat in a wingback chair in the front parlor. He and Rosanna, on the camel back sofa, kept space between them. He'd stopped by to borrow his father's jigsaw. He'd promised the woman who ran the afterschool program at the Y he'd cut her out some animal shapes. He'd return the saw; he had to. Six years after his father's death and no one was allowed to claim mementos.

"You'll fight over cufflinks you have no intention of wearing or garden tools or his final pair of slippers," his mother had told them. "Let me die first, then hate each other."

She had given birth to all nine of them. She could say whatever she wanted. Once his sister Bernice had said, "Mother, you had too many children."

And his mother had said, "Which ones should I not have had?"

"So you met at the university?" his mother now asked. "Roseanne, are you studying for your master's?"

"*Rosanna*," Colin said, but he knew she would not be corrected.

"No," Rosanna said. He'd never seen her shy. It amused him. If he wasn't sitting in his mother's parlor, he might have reached for her, squeezed her hand. "I am a space planner in the facilities department."

"I don't understand."

Rosanna explained.

"You're not an architect though," his mother said. "My daughter Mary Pat is an architect."

"I'm not an architect. No."

"Women can do so many things these days. Even my own daughters surprised me with their ambition. Colin, did you tell her about Kathleen? Kathleen, my oldest, is spokeswoman for the archdiocese."

"I've seen her on television," Rosanna said. "What with the recent scandals and all, I imagine she has a tough job."

Colin hadn't prepared for this. If Rosanna mentioned the questionable canonization of Pius XII, he'd have to get her out in a hurry. He hated to admit it (it had nothing to do with thinking one woman was more suitable than any other) but Maureen knew better than to talk religion with his mother.

"What do we expect in a world where sex is a casual thing? Men loving men, young women . . ." Here his mother paused and turned to an African violet in the window on a starched doily, "giving themselves away to whatever man comes along, with no thought of marriage."

Sometimes, Colin thought, he shouldn't take the passive role with his mother; instead, he should play her game: lay the offensive comment out just as sweetly as you would offer tea. Now, for example, he wished he could chuckle and tell her about the Third Date Rule which his young girlfriend had introduced him to. If you don't sleep with someone by the third date, Rosanna told him, the relationship is doomed. Besides, making out, all the groping, sucking, awkward exchange of body fluids, was more disturbingly intimate according to Rosanna. He had to agree, sex did break the ice.

At the mention of marriage, however, both he and Rosanna grew quiet. She looked down into her hands and stayed that way while Colin tried to change the subject, asking about first one of his siblings then another, a litany of married people, good parents, off on weekends in North Conway or preparing backyards for First Communion parties or using up home equity loans to remodel bathrooms.

"We should go," he said. "We'll go out the back door and pick up the saw."

His mother stood on the top step. She had been married for forty-nine years to the boy next door, the man who made her bed every morning of their lives together, who came downstairs and brewed her tea while she had a bath. They had had too many kids, his sister was right. But Colin knew it was because they wouldn't deny one another. He remembered how, in a house packed with children grabbing fruit off the table, kicking sneakers off on the porch, there were moments when his parents seemed alone, oblivious. His father's burned finger beneath the cold water tap, his mother's head bent over the hand she held, his mother on the chair in their bedroom watching his father hang his tie up on the closet door.

Mostly, he remembered how common it seemed, how easy: that devotion.

What if he told his mother, Maureen wants to try again?

His mother would say what she always said: Go home to your wife.

But their life had a seam that his parents' had not, that his and Rosanna's did not. Not that he and Maureen had lost a child, but that in those days and weeks when their grief was deepest, she had betrayed him.

It didn't rain on their picnic. The sun shone, high clouds sailed, a breeze kicked up dandelion fuzz and discouraged flying insects. Rosanna took off her shoes and picked at fruit salad. Colin pulled conversation from her. He had rare moments like these with her where he felt powerless and afraid. Moments when he thought he must love her or else why worry when she drifted off and he, forced to draw her out, understood how lonely it would be if she decided to leave him. At other times, when he considered life without her, he felt only relief.

She lay back with her knees up so that her skirt fell over them back towards her stomach. He thought of Megan in her little skirts and how he warned her that spinning or cartwheels, or swinging legs would reveal her underwear. But Rosanna was a grown woman, fully capable, he reminded himself, of knowing whether or not she should position herself like that. Maureen hardly ever wore skirts. She preferred jeans, loose sweaters.

But unlike Maureen, Rosanna was not afraid to tell him he wasn't paying enough attention to her. She spelled her needs out clearly whether it was making plans for a date over the phone or whispering in his ear as he made love to her. If she had been unfaithful, he knows she would have cried when she told him, wept, really. Maureen had been so matter-of-fact when she confessed, he couldn't tell what she wanted from him. He hadn't considered reconciliation in the face of such perceived indifference.

She had been similarly straightforward the day she told him they should reconcile. He had not seen it coming. Nothing had changed in their relationship which had been businesslike, efficient. They fought over nothing. They barely spoke except to exchange news of Megan. He had just dropped Megan off, carrying her in because she had fallen asleep on the way home. He lay her on the sofa in the living room, covering her bare legs with the afghan that had always hung over the back of the sofa. Even now, the things that survived their old life surprised him.

"I think we should try again," Maureen said.

As Megan slept, Maureen stood in the dark hallway (she had never before forgotten to leave the light on for them) and claimed it was grief that drove her to do what she did. Women, she said, don't cheat for sex. He hated the word in that context. In all contexts. He didn't consider himself to be someone who had sex. He made love to women. To two women. His wife and, now, Rosanna.

If Rosanna had heard this, she would have said Maureen's theory was crap. He could imagine her saying: "If you don't cheat for sex, why not just meet for coffee?"

He pushed past Maureen and loped down the stairs, uncomfortable as always knowing Maureen watched him go. He considered how pitiful the back of a cuckolded man's head must appear, but when she called him, he turned. It helped him to imagine Rosanna. She was not second prize. He was not settling.

"Colin, please," Maureen had said. "We have a daughter."

He didn't know what Maureen meant. Of course they had a daughter.

"You cheated," he said. "End of story."

Rosanna might never have confessed, Rosanna whose last trip to the confessional had been when she was eleven, a bridesmaid in her cousin's wedding. Why put someone between you and your God? she asked him on an early date, though it wasn't a question. It was something people said when they were twenty-six and had no need for ritual. Rosanna might have lived with her sin and loved him more for it, and he would not have questioned her increased adoration.

She was capable of adoration and, mostly, he felt entitled to it.

"My mother upset you," he said. "I should have warned you about the religion thing."

"You should have warned me about the marriage thing, too, while you were at it."

"I never said I didn't want to get married again."

She had one arm folded behind her head, the other fiddled with the edges of the blanket. "So do you? And if you do, could you see yourself marrying me?"

Maureen didn't ask questions like that. No one he knew asked questions like that.

First comes love, then comes marriage, then comes Rosanna's babies in the baby carriage. That's how he saw those pretend infants of their pretend union: as Rosanna's and not as his own. His own daughter smelled like Maureen, her laundry soap, the damp wallpaper in the Victorian fixer-upper he'd bought with her.

"Don't you want to go to the opera?" he asked.

Rosanna sat up, snapped the lid on her Tupperware bowl and shook her head. "What are you talking about?"

"Go to the opera, vacation in sunny places, eat dinner in fancy restaurants? I want you to do these things, Rosanna. You deserve to do these things. And I can't afford to give you that. I run the YMCA for Chrissakes. I support a child."

She stood and shook out her perfectly clean skirt, swatted its folds and tucked her hair behind her ears so that he could see how her ears stuck out. The first time he'd seen her stepping out of the shower, he'd considered her adorable. Now he felt an overarching sadness that she must not have been a beautiful baby. Not like Megan, her features perfectly proportional; Irish soap baby, Maureen had called her. Even Michael, the brief moment Colin had seen him, had flawless features in his miniature face.

"You want me to say: Oh my God, how unselfish, how altruistic, don't you? Poor, sweet Colin who bears his burdens so magnanimously, but you, my love, are crazy. In-fucking-sane. I've had a dozen or so breakups, but you're the first person to use the cultural-deprivation argument."

Dog walkers and inline skaters glanced at them, Rosanna furiously packing the basket and then tugging at the blanket he still sat on, Colin not thinking quickly enough to rise, then having to roll off and listen to the last part of her speech on his hands and knees. All those boyfriends, he was thinking. He who had only had that one love. If he had only stayed married, his own prudery might never have occurred to him.

"I hate the opera," she said. "And even if I loved it, I can afford my own tickets. I'd never, for example, demand season's tickets and suggest that to afford them we take your daughter out of parochial school. God forbid she should rub shoulders with the great unwashed."

He hated her mentioning Megan. He thought of speaking from where he crouched. But then he sat back on his calves and resisted the urge to grab her arm as she reached for a fork that had landed in the grass. He breathed deeply, repeated it.

"You sound very angry," he said.

Defuse situations, the therapist had said when he finally got up enough nerve to visit one. Anger is a normal, healthy feeling, but avoid meeting anger with anger.

He hadn't felt angry those first few nights after he left. He'd felt pitiful and ashamed. Puzzled, too. After all, he hadn't expected to surround himself with these people—these cheaters and liars and then these people who passed judgment, who didn't recognize pain. His employee? His childhood sweetheart? When he'd shown up at his sisters' houses they'd told him, each in turn: Go home. He'd tried to explain, but they held up a hand to stop him. The last two sisters, most likely having received a call from the first ones he'd visited, never invited him in. They stood behind screen doors as if he stood in an over-sized confessional.

"Whatever it is," they said, "go home and tend to your marriage."

But he hadn't gone home; he'd unlocked the Y and slept on the couch in his office. Slept with his anger and a beach towel he'd picked out of lost and found.

"I let them see how hurt I was," he said to the therapist on his second visit. "But even I had no idea how angry I could become. I never had cause to be angry. I did everything right: married the first woman I loved. Bought the only affordable house in my old neighborhood. Read to my child every night. I didn't deserve what she did to me."

"Let's talk about why this might have happened," the therapist said.

"She took a vow." He cancelled his remaining appointments.

Rosanna, he knew, wouldn't have let him sleep in the car. Him or anyone else. Rosanna and her questions, her insistence on making love with her eyes open. She kept a closet full of spare pillows, handed out house keys to a dozen relatives and friends.

Now she stood, basket in one arm, blanket folded in the other.

"It must be nice," he told her, "to always know exactly what you want."

But this, he realized much later, was probably not the best thing to say.

"It's not the gift you would assume it is," she said. "At least it hasn't been so far."

Her sadness moved him. He wished it could all go away—this conversation, the curious onlookers, his own flashes of indifference.

Rosanna smiled at him, looked at him as his wife never had, such a long stare with so little required of him. He looked away.

"This is the awkward part, see?" she said. "It's not a movie, our life, so instead of me walking away with my stupid picnic stuff, I have to wait until you unlock the car door for me and then we have to ride a few miles in silence and then I have to think of something to say to wrap the scene before I climb out and you drive away."

He hadn't thought that far ahead. He hadn't thought she might cry. She didn't, though her voice thickened.

The first time he'd seen Rosanna she'd been on a bench in a common area of the university where she worked and where he completed the last class for his long delayed graduate degree. She sat beneath an ornamental cherry tree, its buds tight and black. She did not eat or read, was not, he learned later, waiting for anyone. He thought her lovely and a little bit lonely. Though it was probably his own loneliness that made him feel this way. A woman like that, he'd thought, would have a boyfriend. But a few weeks later, he sat beside her anyway and she spoke immediately.

"I've seen you lurking about," she said.

It startled him, that she would use a word like *lurk* to describe his being there.

"I'm taking a class," he said. "Finishing a master's degree. I have to pass this way—"

"And look this way as you pass? And sit a while today before the semester ends and you have no more excuses?" This time she smiled.

Colin felt lucky in a way he hadn't ever felt. Not even when Maureen loved him. Not when Megan was born. These things, he had expected.

On their third date, he sat on her sofa, a huge brown sectional, cushions collapsed at the V. She listened as he told her why his marriage had ended. Not the baby part, not yet. He explained how his wife had had an affair. He wanted it said aloud, to state his shame up front.

Rosanna kissed him. She held his face in her hands. He felt saved, appreciated, and very, very sorry for himself.

He hadn't made love to a woman in over a year. He had never made love to anyone besides Maureen who didn't shave the tops of her legs, whose fine hairs he could still feel under his fingertips. But Rosanna's legs were smooth so that even in the dark he could not pretend she was anyone else, and he did not want to. He stopped often to look at her and she was always looking back.

I can be this person, too, he had thought. Other people can see me and say: This is who he is now. A man who is dating a young, spirited woman. A man to envy, really, things have turned out so well.

When he tried helping her with the picnic supplies she said: "I can manage."

He knew it was true. She had what he called her support system:

good friends, a twin sister, a mother she spoke to daily. Beyond that, she had none of the things he had, the things he managed: a daughter who expected yogurt-covered raisins or feather boas whenever he came to pick her up, who slept in his bed and demanded apple pie for breakfast. Who, at four, had started sucking her thumb. An ex-wife devoid of ambition who waited for her share of his meager paycheck, a woman unwilling to act affected by the destruction she'd caused, a family who still considered him a married man.

He unlocked the car door for Rosanna and she brushed past him, yanking it closed herself. She rolled the window down but stared ahead.

"You don't have to prove anything to me, Rosanna," he said, bending into the open window. "You're a wonderful person. Strong and beautiful and funny. And if you're angry with me, well, that's not my responsibility. You have to feel how you have to feel."

She turned to him, arched her eyebrow and flared her nostrils.

"Feel this," she said, flipping him her middle finger. No one had done that to him since eighth grade. He felt fatherly, embarrassed for this girl who thought her anger might move him, and finally ashamed by how completely he had desired her.

"You know what your problem is?" she said when he had climbed into the driver's seat. "Well, one of them? You've got yourself convinced you're the good guy. You convinced me, too. And I felt sorry for you. Couldn't imagine what kind of a monster would hurt you the way your wife did. But I get it now."

"This is not an appropriate topic for us," Colin said, his heart beating hard, his hands clamped on the steering wheel.

"Now we're into appropriate. We weren't last week. Remember that? Remember fucking in the bathroom at your friend's house before we rejoined the dinner party?"

How to stop her, he wondered? How to make her keep her voice down? People strolled by the window, people whose lives he assumed were more proper, more normal than his own. The kind of people, he thought, I used to be.

"She left you because you shut down, Colin. When she most needed you to respond to her, you turned into some weird reptile-robot-guy, blinking but otherwise immune to stimuli. She felt the way I feel right now. As if you never cared. As if it was all a joke. You wanted to get married, have kids. She was the answer. You wanted to screw someone's brains out, you came looking for me."

Rosanna had taught him things that, in the light of day, made him blush and stammer as if people could read his thoughts, could know why he hadn't gotten much sleep the night before. He wondered what Maureen had felt after making love with Kevin. Though of course he'd never asked her. He'd just gone about his new life, trying to expunge those questions which his passion for Rosanna had helped him to do.

Colin's head pounded. He sweated through his shirt.

"You need to take some responsibility, goddamnit," he said. "I'm far from the first man you've slept with!"

He drove his elbow so hard into the window beside him, he sent a thin vein through the glass.

A runner stopped abruptly and stuck his head through Rosanna's window. "Are you okay here?" he asked.

Rosanna nodded into her lap.

"I can take you home," the man said. "I can call you a cab."

Without looking up, she said: "We've had a terrible fight. But he won't hurt me."

The man leaned in farther and spoke to the side of Colin's face: "Cut the shit, buddy, okay? Calm down already. You're scaring the shit out of her you asshole."

Then he jogged off, turning once to glare at Colin.

———

The day Michael died, the nurse put him in Maureen's arms and left them alone. Maureen, still groggy from the painkillers, whimpered and kissed his forehead. She asked Colin if he wanted to hold him, but Colin had only leaned into her arm and forced himself to stroke the baby's hand, drawing back when he noted its warmth. Maureen had looked at Colin and opened her mouth though she said nothing.

Later, on one of the first Sundays he'd returned Megan to the home he hadn't completely removed his things from, Maureen reminded him of that moment.

"Why didn't you take him?" she asked, and Colin, stiff with indignation, turned to leave without answering.

Maureen called after him: "I thought it was something I could never forgive you for," she said. "I thought it would be impossible to understand why you behaved that way. But I did. I forgave you, Colin. I had no right to take it out of context."

He resisted the urge to break into a run, the street unrolling downhill, the wind burning his eyes, his car parked illegally because he'd known he wouldn't linger.

———

He maneuvered the same car into traffic, careful with his signal light, lifting a hand at the car that let him switch lanes. He prayed for no traffic, no red lights, nothing but clear sailing ahead to Rosanna's apartment. Hoped he hadn't left anything up there he'd feel compelled to retrieve. The idea of being alone in his car again, a car he'd slept in when other workers at the Y became suspicious both of Kevin's abrupt resignation and Colin's wrinkled clothes, his showering in the locker room, his gym bag behind his desk, comforted him.

Rosanna stepped out silently, gathered her things from the trunk and walked away from him, into a world he would never know. What will become of us, he might have asked?

He would return to what he thought he was: a good man, used badly, a father first and then a son. Suddenly, he knew he would also return to his wife and resume what, on the surface, would resemble his old life. He would be nowhere near as happy as those who saw them together again, who believed they had come to their senses, that their marriage was proof of something hopeful for all of them. But every night, he would tuck his daughter in, leave her door open a crack in case she called to him. He would sleep with his back to Maureen for a few weeks and when they finally did make love, he would have to concentrate to block out images of her with a man who was not a stranger to him. She would not whisper to him but would remain silent, perhaps afraid to say the wrong name, and he would never open his eyes again, so carefully would he have to guard against his visions, so precisely would the images of his new world be crafted.

SINGING DONKEYS, HAPPY FAMILIES

Sven Jarlsen was a volunteer with vision, a cook committed to local food, a mother of a man. He wasn't handsome. His nose was too big and his hair, blond and stringy, never looked combed, but when Mags watched him zip his son into his filthy jacket and trot into school with still-warm apple bread for Share Day at Green Hills Arts and Earth Preschool, she swooned.

She told herself it was foolish, the crush, a way to get herself and her three young daughters out of the house each day. But it worked. She was happy. So take that, world! That morning, for example, Mags had hustled her oldest daughter, Jolie, to the bus stop and stood with other mothers who glanced at the scuffed white sandals Jolie insisted on wearing over her striped tights.

"Umm, Mags?" one of them said. Mags could never remember which was which and several were named Katie. "Tuesday is gym day?"

"Are you asking me a question?" Mags said, her face burning. "I mean, it sounds? Like you're asking me a question?"

She also felt like pinching Jolie. The child got an idea in her head and made them all look like fools.

Colleen Duncan, neighborhood peacemaker and happiest wife on the planet, asked if Mags's husband was working from home that morning.

"Not go into the office for a day?" Mags said, chuckling. "A work-aholic like him? You've got to be joking."

But none of the others laughed. Instead, Colleen said, "I only ask because you don't have Tyra and Desa with you."

Mags's two- and three-year-old were, in fact, strapped into booster chairs at the breakfast table licking the frosting off week-old birth-day cake. When she'd tried to force them outside, they'd screamed so loud, she'd decided they'd be happy enough until she got back. Not much of a choking hazard with frosting, either. The other moth-ers, however, had managed to dress all of their toddlers appropriately and to have brushed their own hair before heading out the door.

That's why they don't like me, Mags thought, not exactly wound-ed. What could you expect from people who could be satisfied with so little? A house that looked like every other house in the neighbor-hood and a three-mile walking loop that allowed them to exercise and gossip at the same time. That's why she drove her middle daugh-ter two towns away to pre-school every day, to escape them.

At Green Hills, Tyra's classmates tramped across the parking lot in outfits they had obviously chosen themselves—pink striped shirts with flowered shorts (despite a morning frost), velvet dresses with filthy sneakers, rain boots on this gloriously sunny day. Their hair re-sembled nests of long-departed sparrows. Their noses ran unchecked and no carabiners of antibacterial gel swung from their backpacks. Here, the pathologically disorganized might pass for the creatively permissive, and Mags was sure she could make friends, rejoin the world of adults.

It hadn't been as easy as she'd hoped, but during the final week in October, Sven Jarlsen printed up the fliers asking for volunteers: *Teepee Building Committee*. Mags lingered at the bulletin board pretending to be absorbed in the poster on recognizing and treating head lice, but surreptitiously gazing at Sven's advertisement, envisioning his long, pale fingers, calloused with the folk guitar he strummed on Fridays during Recycled Art Hour, caressing his computer's keyboard.

Yes, thought Mags, who had never built anything in her life, who still called the original teepee builders Indians no matter how many times she'd been corrected, I will help him. Committees promised guilt-imposed roles, but how much delegating would the most resourceful man on the planet do? She couldn't stay home another second pretending to busy herself while unfolded laundry spilled off the couch under which rolled juice cups whose contents solidified before she excavated them. She had only to approach Sven when he dropped off his son.

"Has your daughter been scratching?"

Mags jumped. Miss Pat, lead teacher, was a broad-shouldered woman with a thick cord of gray hair coiled on the top of her head. Around her lingered the same aroma Mags detected in the donkey paddock.

"Oh, no," Mags said as parents drew their children to the opposite side of the crowded hallway, parents who hadn't combed their kids' hair in months. More loudly, she said, "I'm thinking of helping with the teepee."

"Well, check them. Every night." Miss Pat removed an outdated flier for a folkfest, her nails rimmed in black, and moved off.

She doesn't like me, Mags thought, and this time, it did wound. She had seen the woman speak with other moms, had heard her deep-throated laugh, watched her escort them into her office to research some idea for one selfless project or another. Why, oh why, did people say real life was nothing like high school? Surely there was a way to contribute, to prove she belonged here? It wasn't Mags's fault she had no ideas of her own. She was a good follower, however, and believed the value of that role to be seriously undervalued. Tyra ran ahead to the pilly rug and curled up beside a girl in a leopard print leotard and a purple tulle skirt who read aloud from a book. Mags's two-year-old, Desa, pulled boots out of the cubbies, boots that had been there since last winter, and tossed them into the path of parents trying to unload their children. Mags ignored her. Blood inspired her to act, little else.

You can't let one encounter discourage you, Mags reminded herself. Then, remembering the bus stop, she said aloud: "Well two." She had ironed a shirt for this, had squeezed into the pair of jeans most likely to still be stylish. She'd showered and left her hair damp remembering how her husband loved the smell of it freshly shampooed.

When she saw Sven enter, she approached him. "You're Sven, correct?" she said, smiling. For the past two weeks, she'd bleached her teeth using pasty strips that left her smacking her lips for hours after she'd removed the gluey things.

"Why, yes," he said. It was clear he had no idea who she was.

"I'm Mags Dillon, Tyra's mother. I'd like to help with the teepee."

"Excellent," he said, but as she stood there marveling at how sincerely he made eye contact behind his wire-framed glasses, he said no more, no meeting times, no further information. Instead, his son, Erik, approached and said, "I told you I wanted to bring the pumpkin seeds we roasted, but you forgot. You'll have to go home again for them."

"I have to do some errands first," Sven said, one arm on the little boy's shoulder, but the boy shrugged it off.

"It's your fault we've forgotten and now you must make up for it."

Other parents jostled Mags as they passed, but Sven smiled after his son elbowing his way onto the rug.

"Good thing we live nearby," he said, but not to Mags exactly.

One mother mentioned that people were meeting at Emilia's after drop-off. "Just to grab a quick coffee before we start the day," she said.

Mags had no idea if the invitation was for her or for Sven, but thrilled, she said, "Sounds great," as the woman moved off negotiating the swamp of tossed off articles.

Emilia's was run by a Guatemalan couple who sold only fair trade coffee and dry scones. The coffee tasted gritty as soil, but the women oohed and aahed over it and declared it real.

"Not like that watered down crap they serve at Donny D's," one mother said, looking at Mags for affirmation. Flattered, Mags nodded. Desa loved the coffee. After a few sips, she spun around the place with helicopter arms, causing people to look up scowling from their laptops, but none of the Green Hills women seemed to notice and Mags felt included in a group of mothers for the first time since she had been one.

"Wasn't Beth Clark-Jarlsen coming?" a woman named Tiffany asked. She was chair of the Quilt Committee, the first person who had spoken to Mags at Green Hills since Tiffany spent a great deal of time recruiting members to help out with what she claimed was the biggest fundraiser of the year.

One of the women looked up from her knitting. "She's working on a new case," she said.

"Another one?" Tiffany said. "Well, I guess after she forced Sven to abandon his career—not that it was overly lucrative, mind—she has no choice but to make up the difference."

Someone tried to change the subject, the same way she had when Tiffany had commented on Mary Something-or-other, a trust-fund baby who drank too much, but Desa nearly knocked her coffee cup off the table and this derailed her good intentions. Mags was glad. She liked the gossip.

"The Clark-Jarlsens are a sweet couple," another woman said. "So in love and so alike. Ski like crazy. Hike."

"Trust me," Tiffany said. "No family is as happy as they look."

She was a therapist, so she ought to know. What could be better than spending a morning talking about other flawed families? Keep reminding yourself, Mags thought, that everyone looks perfect on the surface. Well, lots of people do.

However, if Sven did feel outdone by his wife, that would explain his dedication to the school. Mags understood how that could fill a void. Anyway, Mags *was* happy with these people. She didn't even mind that one of the women, when her three-year-old tugged at her, lifted up her wool sweater and allowed the child to stand beside her and nurse.

"You're making friends," her husband Tom said, when he placed his daily 11:45 call to her from the big, giant world of his office. Mags hummed as she dumped another pile of laundry onto the sofa. In the morning, she'd ferret through it for what they needed.

A few days later, Tiffany said the same group of moms would be meeting at the playground for lunch once school was out.

"We pack lunches, beach blankets," she said.

When Tom called just as she was running out the door to pick up Tyra and follow the caravan to the playground, he said, "Another invitation? I guess it wasn't a fluke."

Mags didn't understand.

"I didn't mean anything by it," said Tom. "Just that sometimes, people don't get invited back."

"It's not an interview," Mags said. "It's just a group of nice people. Why shouldn't I be included in that?"

He told her she was making too big a deal of what he said. But Mags could tell he was surprised, and she was angry that she'd remember that during what she had thought would be a nice day.

As it turned out, Mags couldn't spend a lot of time thinking about anything. She also had no chance to sit on the blanket and hand feed her daughters tiny bites of whole wheat sandwiches, because

Desa sprinted from one amusement to the next, hurtling her small body up the climbing structure that, at its tallest point, had no railing along one side. Tiffany marveled at Desa's athleticism, but Mags fumed. How was she supposed to make friends if she couldn't sit down for a second? She had wanted to relax on the blanket, to have her daughter braid her hair as she sat in the sun the way the nursing mother's child did now. That's what happens when you give up breastfeeding after only a few half-hearted attempts, Mags thought. Formula babies have no attention span.

Tiffany must have noticed her gazing at the blanket because she said, "Harder for the lice to take hold."

"Lice?" Mags cringed.

"Scourge of Green Hills. Someone keeps bringing them in but we haven't quite figured out who it is yet."

Mags wondered if any of the mothers had overheard the teacher questioning her, but they, too, must have noted how the children bent their heads together as they examined scabs or collaborated on collages. Some children wore winter caps already, and friends mugged it up trying them on, too.

"I'm sure it's not any one family," Mags said.

"Perhaps," Tiffany continued. "Anyway, there are a lot worse things that can happen to your child than lice so, no biggie, really. I mean, you just have to bag all the stuffed animals and pillows for a couple weeks and wash everything—and I mean *everything* in your house."

Mags's head pounded. In a world as barely held together as hers, how would she ever summon the resources to combat parasites?

By the time Sven called the first meeting of the teepee crew, Mags had forgotten her whiter smile and wet hair trick. She had dashed out of the house with a feverish Desa, with Tyra on ibuprofen to wipe out signs of her own illness.

Desa whined on Mags's hip, lay a hot head against her mother's neck.

"Soon as we get home, you get medicine, too," Mags promised. "Then you and Mommy go nighty night."

She had slept less than an hour the night before. Even when Tom got up to soothe the girls, they clamored for her. Finally, she ignored them, but still. At least Mags would have an excuse for missing the first Quilt Committee meeting. She pulled on sweat pants—she'd pretend she worked out—and dragged a reluctant Tyra into the building just as Sven was leaving.

"Ah," he said, stepping forward as if to hug her. He had been whistling.

Mags stopped, Tyra's sleeve pinched in her fingers, the child's arm raised so far from her body, she couldn't negotiate the muddy walkway.

"Please, Mommy," Tyra said. "You're hurting me."

Sven looked startled, and anger surged through Mags at her daughter's poor timing. "Let me help," he said, lifting Tyra across a particularly muddy patch. Would Tom have done that? How could she know when he had never ventured into this place he called *her* world.

"It's not my world," Mags had said, ruffled. "It's Tyra's."

Tom had peered at her over the tops of the reading glasses he had recently begun wearing though she doubted he needed them yet. "You know what I mean, dear," he said. Dear. As if she was a hundred years old already.

After Sven set Tyra down and patted her head, he turned to Mags: "We're meeting today," he said. "One o'clock."

"Today," Mags said. "Yes. Oh."

She looked down at her daughter whose nose ran over her chapped lips. Tyra scratched her head, studied her fingernails before tasting them.

The Quilt Committee didn't meet until 3. Surely Mags could be out of there by the time they arrived. There was just the small problem of her sick children. Sven stood as if he had all day to wait for her reply.

She smiled. "Shall I meet you here then?" she asked. He said that would be grand.

Mags left her girls, double-dosed on fever medicine, at her neighbor's house, showered quickly and then, desperate to cure her own increasing headache, sucked down the remaining children's ibuprofen and, fearing that wouldn't work, gulped some old cough medicine as well. She brewed a small pot of coffee and drank two cups, black. Sven would bring Erik. Other parents, too, would include their children in another of those let's-involve-the-kids nightmare projects where every adult idea is squashed by a child's inane input—we can make a drawbridge that really works! let's get a few ponies to tie out front!—and nothing gets done. But Mags needed to appear calm. She could be a Zen parent, but only without her children. At her neighbor Colleen's, the girls dove into a tub of Barbies and barked for apple juice. No one at Green Acres would have Barbies, Mags was pretty sure, and the apple juice would be organic, but Mags smiled and said to Colleen, "I love you. Oh! I mean I owe you."

"No problem," Colleen said. "You seem awfully excited about this."

Colleen was one of the most intimidating mothers Mags knew, creative, compulsively neat. She spouted off about her husband's foibles as if being colorblind or shopping at the local drugstore for her birthday were the most adorable things she could think of. Mags longed to confess her crush to someone, but not anyone who baked the kinds of theme birthday cakes this woman did.

Desa tugged on Mags's leg. "Head hot," she said, using Barbie's arm to scratch it.

Mags bent down and ruffled her baby's hair. Her hands shook wildly. "Mommy won't be long," she said, in the kind of voice she had only ever used with a prospective employer's puppy. "This is a very important thing she has to do." To Colleen she said, "Volunteering for a worthy cause makes me feel so filled." Then she paused, buzzing a bit from the medicine and giggled. "*Ful*-filled."

After a pause, Colleen laughed a bit, too.

Only two other people were under the tree outside the goat enclosure when Mags arrived. One was Daisy, the young woman who lived in a trailer on school property and fed the animals. Fowl erupted whenever she walked by. She smelled like grain and something sharp and revolting that Mags assumed was goose shit. Erik and two other children played around the adults, mimicking the rooster's strut, the braying of the miniature donkeys. It would have been aggravating, but Mags's head swam with over-the-counter narcotic and the dark brew. She beamed, clasping her hands in her lap, as Sven described the process.

Daisy had a good idea where to secure affordable duck.

"Affordable duck," Mags said, snorting. But no one else got the joke.

"I have to go worm the horse," Daisy said, and left them, the emaciated dog trotting at her heels, the barnyard exploding in quacks.

The other person, a man who looked too old to be the father of the infant slung across his chest, suggested Native American cave painting images. He would research which ones would best convey harmony and friendship.

"Cool," said Sven.

That didn't sound like such a great contribution to Mags who had yet to be assigned something and who had no idea what to offer since she knew as much about building teepees as she did about skinning elk. If you did skin an elk.

The nursing mother—Emily, Mags learned, as the men called out greetings to her—came late, her three-year-old sulking and yanking on her sweater as she plopped on the ground and pulled him into her lap. Her other child joined the group of older children, proclaiming loudly that she was the farmer and would chase them which produced more ear-splitting screams. The men joked about the ongoing construction projects at Emily's ancient house. Sven said he'd come over and help with a plastering job. The other man gave her advice as to where she could find antique bricks. Mags felt a pang of jealousy. She had come here hoping to make some friends, but she would always be left out of the lives of these hippie people. No matter how she tried to ingratiate herself, her husband would no sooner fit into this group than he would know how to milk one of those goats. If you did milk a goat.

Emily had a sewing machine that she used to repair sails. "I can make the smoke flaps," she said, and this thrilled everyone.

What, exactly, would they *do* with a teepee, anyway? It suddenly sounded like the most ridiculous idea Mags had ever heard and she wondered how she could be attracted to a man with so much time on his hands. Her own husband worked long hours and made tons of money that she had no idea how to spend. Wasn't that preferable to someone handy enough, idle enough, to build play structures? But then Sven leaned back on his arms, stretched his legs out in Mags's direction and said, "And what will we have sweet Mags do?"

He hadn't said sweet to anyone else.

"Whatever," Mags said. Her tongue darted out to lick her lips. What if, God forbid, he asked *her* to sew something?

"Mags and I will search for poles," Sven announced. "Saplings tall enough and firm enough to wrap canvas around."

"Saplings are my specialty," crowed Mags, steeped once more in infatuation.

Just as they stood up, a battered Saab turned into the driveway and a woman stepped out. She wore a gray wool sweater, jeans and the kind of shoes you wouldn't have to change out of if, say, you had to ford a river. Sven smiled widely and wrapped one arm around her as if she was the world's greatest show and tell exhibit.

"This is a surprise," he said.

"A surprise?" she said. "It's Erik's therapy day. You didn't think I'd let him miss it for *this*, did you?" Mags couldn't be sure, though it seemed the woman shuddered.

"Mom's right," Erik said, climbing into the front seat and rolling down the window. "It's stupid to build a teepee, Dad. It's not a great idea."

The other members of the committee busied themselves fussing with their children. Mags flicked detritus off her toes. Sven mumbled something, and the car drove off.

When no one spoke for several seconds, Mags blurted: "Now, where were we? Oh, right, the sapling search."

But it took a few seconds before Sven returned from staring after his wife's tail lights.

The search would begin in the Parson's Woodlot, several dense acres of forest that bordered the school, but far enough away so that they would not be subjected to the honking of geese or to the braying of miniature donkeys. Mags had worn flip flops.

"Will you be all right in those?" Sven asked. How could any woman dismiss a man with this kind of awareness?

Mags thanked him for his concern. "Tough feet," she said.

The man with the infant sling had headed over to the library. Emily's son, on his knees beside his mother, had wiped his milky mouth on her sleeve.

Mags followed Sven through the parking lot as he loped ahead, head bowed, steps less sprightly than usual. Suddenly, Mags could see him as an old man, shoulder bones protruding through his t-shirt, the knobs and ridges of his skull visible, his cheekbones poking out from under his glasses. An old man, Mags thought, whose misfortune it had been to love a cold woman, to raise a son who had grown up believing in himself and had turned that into a life lived selfishly. It had nothing to do with what kind of a parent you were, or what kind of person for that matter. You tried marriage, you did the best you could with kids, and then you moved on to the next thing with the weighted realization that all your hard work had earned you nothing but a reminder that you are a member of the animal kingdom, an efficient spawner or a necessary fertilizer, critical for the survival of the species. As clear as this appeared to her, poor Sven had no idea, toiled away in earnest investing in the life he believed he had engineered.

Suddenly, she felt so sorry for this man who deserved to be loved, that she grabbed his hand, and he turned, his expression curious. After several confused beats, he squeezed. They stood for a moment like that, linked beneath a canopy that speckled them both. Then Mags took one step towards him and he leaned forward as if to help her across the hard-packed earth just as Tiffany's car turned into the drive for the Quilt Committee meeting at 3. In broad daylight, Mags and Sven froze in the Volvo's safety headlights.

When she arrived home, Mags was surprised to see Tom's car in the garage. Surprised and then terrified. How had he heard? And, really, what was there to hear? It had been a gesture, not an act. But Tiffany's face had blanched behind the windshield. Mags had stammered a hello once she'd dropped Sven's hand, but the woman had fumbled with a box in her hatchback and had used the task to avoid any more contact with them. Mags called out that she'd be at the next meeting. To sign her up for something! as brightly as she could manage. Not bright, Mags thought, as she drove away, the sapling search postponed, her hands shaking on the wheel. Manic.

Now, she hesitated to open her front door. She would appear as if she had just returned from the best-mother-committee meeting with so many insignificant responsibilities, they would cripple her relationships for months to come. Tom towered over her in the doorway, one side of his shirt untucked, his tie loosened, his hair disheveled. Behind him, stood Tyra, Desa, and Jolie, naked except for the towels draping their shoulders. Their hair was wet, half of Jolie's long strands caught in the purple banana clip on the top of her head. As soon as they saw her, all three howled.

"How could you do this, Mags?" Tom said over the noise. She thought he might cry. She had only ever seen him do that on their wedding day and it had hardened her a little, one thin marbled vein. "Do you have any idea how embarrassing this is? How absolutely irresponsible? Our neighbors may never talk to us again."

She had a moment to admire the speed at which Tiffany must have delivered Mags's condemnation, but then she felt nothing but fear. However her husband had learned of her actions didn't matter. "I'm sorry," she said, her throat beginning to close. "I didn't mean anything by it. It was just a stupid fantasy."

"A fantasy? A *fantasy*? What kind of nonsense are you spouting? Colleen was right. You *have* been drinking! Look at your daughters. Look at me! Do you feel any remorse at all?"

Despite her dissatisfaction with motherhood, she had beautiful children. Not rude like Erik or needy like the nursing preschooler. As much work as it was to care for them, she loved how Desa's feet were still fat, how Jolie twisted her hair when she was very tired, how Tyra sang all day without realizing she was doing it. She had read once that it wasn't necessary to be a great mother, just to be good enough, and the idea had buoyed her for weeks after. I can do that! she told herself, and maybe she had. With help, of course, from a normal husband who went to work all day and returned to a houseful of females that naturally baffled him.

"It was the stupidest thing I've ever done," she said. "I mean, he's a sweet man and his wife is so cold and I admit, I was attracted to him, but I also felt so *sorry* for him." She started to cry. "I would never have pursued anything. I don't know what Tiffany told you. I've heard she can be a gossip, but I was just trying to be nice. I swear that's all it was."

Where she expected more public, Hester-Prynne-ish chastisement from her husband, she received only silence though it took her a moment to realize he hadn't spoken since the girls still wailed. Why were they naked, she wondered? Why the strange hairdo? Jolie reached her hand up and raked her fingers across her scalp which increased her volume just as the pieces came together in Mags's mind. Tom hadn't heard about Sven at all. Her daughters had lice.

The chemical shampoo, a poison, was useless, the natural stuff ridiculously expensive and impossible to find. Olive oil with a drop of tea tree beneath a shower cap seemed most effective and most accessible, but the girls cried so hard because of the smell, Tyra threw up all over her bedroom floor, Desa cut her own hair, and Jolie regressed to baby talk. Three days into the siege, the washing machine ground its guts so loudly, Mags thought a plane might be spiraling out of the sky, heading for their deck. She considered running outside and positioning herself just so.

"Bearings are shot," the repairman said. "Cost less to replace it." He offered to call a friend at the local appliance store to see what was on sale. "They could probably deliver you something by tomorrow."

Mags got so teary, she had to look away. It was the first kind thing anyone had done for her since she had aroused everyone's lurid suspicions and had infected several public school classrooms and her neighbor's house with a dreaded parasite and a tenacious fever. Tom shaved his own non-infected head and stopped often at the pharmacy for more supplies, wordlessly dropping off the bag on the counter and busying himself at his computer until it was time to pick up the pizza or the Chinese or the subs. If only Mags could have enjoyed those several nights of not cooking, but it was harder to swallow when you were ignored than it was if you were stared at.

"You can't tell me you've never had a crush on someone else. A teensy, harmless infatuation?" she had said that first night as she lay in their bed in a pink showercap, her scalp tingling from the tea tree. "It doesn't mean I don't love you. I would never have *acted* on it." It was absurd, now, the notion of Sven as some kind of romantic lead, though the sensation of his hand leaving hers, the absence of that heat, stayed with her. "And I wasn't drinking. I'd just had cough medicine. A lot of it. And some coffee. Two cups."

Without turning towards her, Tom said, "And all this is supposed to make me feel better? The fact that my wife is attracted enough to another man that, to be with him, she overdoses on cough medicine and leaves our sick, lice-infested daughters at a friend's?"

"She's not my friend," Mags said. "None of these people are my friends."

But Tom told her he had no time for self-pity so she didn't explain why that spark of interest in another man, that flicker of possibility, had been so important for all of them. How it had gotten her out of bed each morning, how it had allayed an unnameable fear.

Her only friend was the school nurse who had called Mags at home after Jolie's third day out of school. Mags wouldn't have told her the truth, but Jolie herself answered and admitted tearfully why she had to stay home. When Mags finally yanked the phone away from her, she heard the nurse burble, "Oh, sweetie, just tell Mummy to bring you in. I'll check you all out."

When Mags did visit twenty minutes later, the woman hugged her. "You poor thing," she said. "All three?"

"And me, too." Mags collapsed in the tiny chair beside the desk and took the proffered box of tissues into her lap.

"The phone calls I get!" the nurse sighed. She was a large woman, ample-chested, dressed in a cardigan with colored leaves appliquéd onto it. She stood over Jolie's head and combed. "As if it's my fault the school can never quite get the buggers to go away. I tell them all they have to do is comb, but no one wants to do the *work*."

"You mean, they're here, too?" Mags said.

The nurse laughed. "My dear, they're *everywhere*! You didn't think you invented the darn things, did you?"

When she had finished checking all the girls and Mags, she brandished a clean comb: "You did it!" she said. "You see? It *can* be done!"

Mags stood up straight, an example to other mothers, and marched off to the beauty salon for a cut, color (hair dyes, the nurse told her, repelled the critters) and eyebrow wax.

By the time she returned to Green Hills, Tom had begun grunting in her direction. The girls had rediscovered plastic toys and had stopped demanding their stuffed animals. Everything works out, she said to herself in her new friend, the nurse's, voice. Every crisis is temporary.

Geese blocked the school's driveway. Cars lined the road as parents shepherded their children past traffic. Mags was happy to be back, part of the stream of people with agendas. She tried to make eye contact with Emily, the nursing mother, an eye-roll of shared hilarity: *those wacky animals!* but Emily was, as usual, too fixated on her brood. Or maybe she doesn't recognize me, Mags said, tossing her stylish blunt cut. Daisy, trying unsuccessfully to herd the geese, had enough on her mind. But Tiffany, too, turned away just as Mags raised her hand to say hello.

She's told them, Mags thought.

Miss Pat marched out to see what the trouble was, the bony dog trailing her. Mags smiled at her hopefully, but Miss Pat took one look at Mags's haircut and Desa's uneven, cropped do, and her nostrils flared.

"Your daughter will have to be cleared by your pediatrician before returning," she said. "And it's about time. Do you have any idea how long we've been trying to find the source of this infestation?"

Two mothers in the coffee/playground group looked up from

negotiating through geese shit, then pressed their heads together murmuring.

Because he was late, Sven had a space closer to the building when he pulled in. The passenger side door opened and Beth emerged, dressed in hiking clothes as was her husband. The little boy pointed at the noisy scene. His parents watched him, Sven grinning, Beth crossing her arms. Perhaps Mags had crossed the line with Sven and now she had to suffer the recriminations. He was married, after all, as was she. But original lice culprit? Her indignation rose. She turned to Miss Pat and leaned close to the woman's face so the squawking would not drown her out.

"They *have* been cleared," she said. Miss Pat took a step back, but Mags matched it. "By a much better woman than anyone here. If you really want to be safe, why not check *all* these filthy heads?"

On her hip, Desa squirmed and Mags, hands steady, set her down.

"How dare you," Miss Pat began, but Desa had taken off, arms pinwheeling. The honking, spitting creatures scattered. In their paddock, the donkeys brayed and kicked their stumpy legs. The goats darted back and forth bawling, and chickens scattered into the woods. The dog barked, nipping goose feathers and people's ankles. Tyra released her mother's leg and joined her sister and then the other children did too, the school yard filled with a cacophonous explosion of running and waddling bodies, flapping wings and jackets, and parents desperate to catch something, yelping when the dog made contact.

Miss Pat screamed over the noise, "Look what you've done!"

Mags did look over the top of the chaos to where Sven stood. His wife attempted uselessly to catch their son, but Sven tossed his head back and laughed. This made Mags laugh, too, and when he finally looked at her, she remembered how for one moment, she had been awash in light. Remembered, too, what she had not imagined—that *she* had dropped *his* hand, and that, even after she did so, his arm had hung out there for an unnatural pause as if asking why it should not return.

Later this morning, as Mags walked from clean room to clean room of her house, fearful of the next hour, the one after that, the children would gather to make salt dough, the mothers to drink Fair Trade coffee and stitch quilt squares, Sven and his wife to make love on a rarely used trail, surprised at their own daring. It would be as if none of this had ever happened, as if Mags herself had never existed, the small world righted, gathered into its flocks and herds, into its easily disrupted gaggles.

ON BEING LONELY AND OTHER THEORIES

Officer Jon Olvey thought his last stop would be at Reans' Diner where Chuck Robideau hadn't sobered up much over his coffee and banana cream.

"Hasn't paid for it," Dick Rean said when Jon walked in. "Only orders pie when he knows you'll show up before he has to pay."

There are times, especially with Shar—the sounds of breaking waves from the end of her street—when he considers leaving these people whose addresses are motels and campgrounds, whose kids steal away from field day to rifle through teachers' desks for cash.

"What good's a cop if he doesn't have any policing to do?" his father had said when Jon could not find work in other towns and had joined the local force, instead. His buddies had fled after high school, but Jon's father said, "Why head off to some rich town to chase after drunk prom goers and gardeners who ignore water bans?"

Finally, Jon had agreed. It was hard to imagine doing anything for the next forty years, but if he had to do something, he'd like to mix it up. Get inside trailer homes and carnival quarters, into million-dollar seaside retreats. Rage, grief, the many distortions of passion, altered people in ways he had not expected. And, though he'd only admitted it to his wife, Vicki, he felt good about what he did.

"It's like I make a difference," he said, emboldened by the darkness of their bedroom.

Vicki told him it meant he'd found something worthwhile to do with his life. "We made the right decision," she said. "Staying here to raise our kids."

Only lately did he consider what else there might be.

He tossed Chuck Robideau into a holding cell and climbed into his car. He'd be home late, but with a legitimate excuse this time, not like the night before when he'd fallen asleep at Shar's until three. He turned the ignition. Nothing. Piece of shit battery, piece of shit car that was a gift from his father-in-law who had acted as if he was giving a kid up for adoption.

Vaughn Whelan, Vicki's cousin—the town was full of cousins, fathers who had married a few times, mothers who had married a few more creating a ganglion of family relations—gave Jon a lift to the DARE van which was parked in front of the elementary school.

"Might as well take it," Vaughn said, though he didn't sound convinced. When Jon was a kid, racing up and down the strip, Vaughn had fixed a few tickets for him. Now, Vaughn waited to make sure Jon got off okay.

"Have to be back here tomorrow morning anyway," Jon said.

Then, as Jon leaned into the window to thank Vaughn, the older man said, "Watch yourself burning the candle at both ends. Don't want anyone to get hurt."

Maybe Vaughn was a better cop than Jon gave him credit for. Vaughn might be Vicki's relative, but he had known Jon's father since elementary school. He looked away and said, "I'll follow you out."

Jon sped past the mini golf, paint flaking off the T-Rex, past Clam Hut II whose lights were off, past Seashell Cottages, rows of pink cabins full of petty thieves and alcoholics. The van smelled of Shar's vanilla perfume, the Chapstick she drew on compulsively. They had used the van for the kind of quickies Jon could never have imagined with his wife. What would Vicki do with the kids if he called and said, "Meet me for my break at 8?" She'd say he was out of his mind. She'd be right, but how was he supposed to resist the anticipation of shoving a skirt up a woman's thighs as she moaned in his ear? He was so aroused thinking about it, he had to see Shar. He was already late. What difference would another hour make?

As he made the U-turn, he glimpsed something big-shouldered and brown just before he heard the thud. The impact tossed the animal against the curb where it lay, one paw resting on the sidewalk. When he approached it—a brindled pit bull—it whimpered, but when Jon tried to touch it, it snapped, blood bubbling out its jaws.

Vaughn loped up beside him.

"Kill it?" he asked.

Jon shook his head. The dog shuddered and Jon wondered if his shaking hand on its massive shoulders would quiet it. Vaughn offered to call animal control and Jon envisioned Bose Clock, the ancient dog catcher, boiling water for his instant coffee before he set out from the last house in town, several miles away. Stupid fucking town, Jon thought. Stupid fucking killer dogs off leash.

"I'll drive it to the vet myself," Jon said. "If I can just get the thing in the van without losing an arm."

"If you say so," Vaughn said. "Closest place is that new one on Central."

Shar's house was less than a mile from there. Jon could see her after he dropped the dog off, before he headed back to the station to write the report. As he lifted the dog, easily eighty pounds, Vaughn kept his belt cinched around the animal's jaws. After Jon set the dog inside the van and stepped into the streetlight, Vaughn pointed out the blood on his shirt.

"Bleeding out his ear," Vaughn said. "Not good."

Jon patted the animal's neck, felt its heartbeat, noted the tag on its collar.

"Hang in there, bud," he said.

Vaughn studied Jon as if he was going to say something, but instead, he patted Jon's back and took off without his belt.

Why Jon had not expected the answering service at the vet's, he had no idea, but it pissed him off. It'll do that to you—the possibility of a woman waiting just around the block—make you senseless with one-mindedness. Despite the injured dog, Jon's hard-on returned.

"I'll send Dr. Murgo down immediately," the answering service said. "Don't move."

Jon pictured this stranger, Murgo, groping for glasses, clothing, car keys. He had time to surprise Shar, to push open her door and, without a word, shove her up against the wall. What if he had married Shar, if that had been a possibility ten years ago? Would she greet him as hungrily as she did now?

Minutes later, the scene with Shar unfolded as he had hoped, his sleepy girlfriend so dazzled with this surprise that, before he could grab her, she grabbed him, laughing when she reached for his crotch and discovered how happy he was to see her.

Dr. Murgo who, it turned out, lived atop her clinic, was an insomniac.

"I've been here an hour," she said. She was a tiny woman, athletic. She reminded Jon of those girls from high school who didn't like you copying from their lab reports. "I thought you called on your way over."

Jon stammered—tough getting the dog in the vehicle, useless call to the animal control officer. As he spoke, he unlatched the back of the van and was greeted by the smell of dog shit.

"Hold this." Murgo handed him a flashlight and leaned in as if she smelled nothing more than the perfumed heat puffing from her dryer vent. She held the stethoscope to the dog's chest, then un-clamped it from her ears.

"Dead," she said. "Doesn't take long if the animal has internal injuries."

"So there was nothing much we could have done to save him?"

"Except maybe getting here on time."

Pudding was a pit bull with a record: excessive barking, fornicating on the beach, snapping at a pizza delivery kid. Back at the station, Jon called the owner, Clinton Parish, whose file also bulged with pet-ty stuff—shoplifting at the FastMart, trespassing on state property with a metal detector. Drunk and disorderly was a given.

"I'm calling about your dog," Jon said to the man who answered after several rings.

"My what?" he snapped. Then he paused. "My dog?" The gruff-ness disappeared. He hung up before Jon told him what had hap-pened or that the body was at the vet's.

Parish shuffled into the police station, keeping one hand in the pock-et of an ancient Miami Dolphins jacket.

"Come for my dog," he said.

Jon explained what happened—leaving out the delayed trip to the vet's.

"Dead?" Parish asked. Jon nodded, his face burning. Parish set his filthy head on the desk and sobbed.

Jon put a hand his back. "I'm sorry," he said, surprised by the sharpness of the man's shoulder blade.

Even after Jon scrubbed the van with Lestoil and left it open overnight, it stunk. The next morning, he drove a squad car to the elementary school to teach Shar's class about Halloween safety. The idea of seeing her made him jog across the parking lot as if he was twenty minutes late instead of early. Just as the secretary buzzed him in, however, Manfred Mancini, the principal, stepped into the hallway.

"DARE van's missing," he said.

Jon told him it was in for a tune-up.

"I don't want a chair moved in this building without my knowledge." Mancini's true ambition was to be a high school principal. Pre-K to 6 was a waste of good suits. There were no coaches to have coffee with.

"Someone should have told you," Jon said. He didn't mean it. The van was police business.

"I've had the vice principal question every teacher in the building."

Mancini's secretary, Hedda Horn, leaned through the office doorway, her large head of gray hair shaped like a mushroom. "Stan just phoned from his stakeout. He needs to go to the bathroom."

"Closet in Hall B," Mancini told Jon. "Some kid lit the bathroom on fire there yesterday. Started another one in a cafetorium wastebasket last week."

"Arson?" Jon frowned. "You should report that to the chief."

Mancini shook his head. "Situation's under control."

Jon shrugged, closing the door behind him and nearly bumping into Hedda. Jon knew nothing about fashion, but he had an idea that stirrup pants were out and that Hedda shouldn't have worn them even when they were the rage.

"I had the Halloween thing at ten," she said.

Later in the teachers' lunchroom, Hedda would back up her suspicions about Jon and Shar with the evidence of his early arrival. Beneath his buzz cut, his scalp puckered. Why can't Johnny read? he thought. Because everyone in the school is a goddamned detective.

"Chronically early," he said. "Sue me."

"Speaking of lawyers," Hedda called. "Heard you killed my cousin's dog last night."

When he arrived in Shar's doorway, she looked up from inspecting some masterpiece and smiled. Her front teeth overlapped, the one on top a shade yellower than the one on the bottom. She wore glasses, the same marbly brown as a librarian's, and had pulled her hair up with an elastic.

The only kid not craning his neck toward Jon was his son Matthew who studied a clay figure in his hand. A dolphin, Jon guessed. Or a blue whale. The only thing on Matthew's Santa list the year before had been a wetsuit which he wore to swimming lessons. He was a terrible swimmer—hesitant, a violent kicker—but he'd watched every video in several libraries on the *Calypso*. Vicki had had to track more down from branches over the border in New Hampshire.

Jon was proud of his kid but a little unnerved, too. Where did it come from, this freakish command of a subject? Neither he nor Vicki even had something you could call a hobby. Their daughter cut the curtains up with scissors, clogged the toilet washing Barbie clothes; the baby howled before sinking into an unreliable sleep, but Matthew only withdrew into his undersea world.

When Jon had started at the school a year ago, Matthew met him at the door each time and led him in, made him examine his detailed drawings of a Portuguese man o'war. But that was before Matthew ended up in Shar Dulcie's room. Jon tried, but couldn't summon the memory of the first time his son had ignored him. Initially hurt, Jon had described Matthew's behavior to Vicki, hopeful it was one of those stages of development she had heard about from the mothers she spent her days with.

"He hasn't said anything to me about being upset," Vicki said. "Hasn't acted like it, either."

When Vicki turned to Jon, he looked away. The boy could not know. Smart as the kid was, he didn't have ESP. "Probably just embarrassed in front of his friends," Jon said. Though Matthew had no friends.

"Here's an idea," Vicki said. "Ask him."

He hadn't.

Now Jon stood before Shar's students, a bag of glow sticks in his hand. Shar whispered, her face close to his: "You shaved. I love your morning face."

He heard *love* and his head throbbed. He forgot why he'd come, peeked inside the bag and memory returned in a hot rush.

"Everyone take a seat," he said, his voice hoarse.

They sat pretzel-legged before him. When Matthew continued at his table, Shar put her hand on his shoulder and murmured to him. The boy shrugged the teacher's hand off and collapsed outside the semicircle.

"I'm going to be Jason," one kid said. "From *Friday the Thirteenth*." Jon had arrested his father the week before after a domestic incident. He'd burned the ends of his girlfriend's hair with a cigarette lighter.

Dylan Rean, from the same family who owned the diner, was going to be a Ninja. There were dozens of Reans, one more colorless and emaciated than the next.

"I know someone who's going to be Jacques Cousteau," Jon said. "Who knows who Jacques Cousteau is?"

"Maybe a cooking guy?" said the kid in a wheelchair.

Shar had pulled up a small chair beside Jon.

"Jacques Cousteau," Jon said, "is famous for undersea exploration, a real-life superhero."

Matthew refused to flick his eyes in his father's direction but he did look up when Stan Verran appeared in the doorframe and motioned for Shar. Verran, a twenty-something triathlete, had been hired as the vice principal the previous spring. Shar had observed that Stan, unlike most other men in public education, knew enough not to wear short-sleeved shirts with ties. They stood nearly touching shoulders and though the conversation turned quickly serious, there was a moment of familiarity—a quick laugh that could only have derived from some ongoing joke—that made Jon feel queasy.

It took him a moment to look away when he heard Matthew say, "Why are you staring at her?"

"I didn't think you were talking today." Jon sounded meaner than he meant to.

"She's not your girlfriend," Matthew said, and guilt compounded Jon's nausea. He had been here so often lately, assuming, of course, that seven-year-olds were not quite as intuitive as Hedda Horn and her gossipy lunchmates, but sometimes, when he thought the children were busy, he flicked the bare skin of Shar's arm or leaned in to whisper to her. If someone as thick as Hedda suspected them, why not a child as bright as Matthew?

Jon rested his hand on his son's head and remembered how careful he had been not to touch the soft spot there when Matthew was brand new, how his pulse had beat visibly in it and how it had terrified Jon. He leaned down. "Of course she's not my girlfriend," he said. "Don't worry about silly things like that."

"I'm not worried," Matthew said, his brow darkening. "I'm only saying."

When Shar returned and plopped down beside him, Jon stood to gain some space and sent the kids back to their desks to draw a picture of someone who was being a safe trick-or-treater.

As their chatter rose, he looked down at Shar. "What was that all about?"

"The fire was set around 10 yesterday morning. Stan wants a list of kids who left the room. They've targeted a few boys: Dylan; the new kid just because we have no idea what's going on with him; and Jason himself, Cory Bradley. Poor kid has such grief at home. Stan's been trying to take some extra time with him."

"Stan's a really helpful guy. Real sensitive," Jon said. He crossed his arms. Shar snorted and he asked what she found so amusing.

"You're jealous," she said. "The Mister who has a Missus waiting at home for him."

———

Jon told Vicki he'd take Matthew for a haircut and pizza.

Vicki paused over the dishwasher where she rearranged everything so tightly, no space existed for so much as a butter knife.

"You mean get take out?" she said.

Jon said no, they'd eat there. If she didn't need him to bring something home for her and the girls.

"Not at all," she said, straightening up and kissing him hard on the lips. "He'll love it!"

When she walked away, he felt the imprint of her chin against his, licked the taste of her hazelnut coffee off his lips.

Shar had plans anyway. Jon tried to suppress the images of her and Stan that pulsed in his mind. Sometimes she claimed to be busy so she could be alone, someone capable of not waiting for him. He knew because he cruised by in the unmarked car. Never told her because what good would it do to embarrass her? Besides, what else could he give her? Leave his wife and kids, and then pay for them for the rest of his life? So many overtime details he'd see Shar less often than he did now? And if she wanted to have kids he'd have to tell her no. He was done with that. But he never wanted to have that discussion, to have to disappoint her, to say she couldn't have what she deserved.

Did he love her? She'd never asked and, if she had, he would not have answered which Shar would have said was an answer after all. She was sillier, more intelligent than any other girl he'd been with. She had theories: Redheads have a certain smell. Unpleasant. Not all redheads, but the ones with lots of freckles. People who live near a coast are more likely to be introspective. All that soothing motion, that view of infinity. She told him that women who get involved with married men have been lonely since childhood. A chronic loneliness that only brief, unpredictable meetings can temporarily allay. He said not to talk about it anymore.

"Well," she had said, as she started to dress, "when you're not here, I store up a lot to tell you."

He told Matthew they'd eat dinner then go to the beach. It was warm enough, and the kid would wander off in search of shells. When he found something, he'd return with the explanation, maybe a Latin name for it. Jon stopped at the station to pick up his paycheck. Vaughn met him in the parking lot.

"Chief's asking for you," he said. "About the dog." It took Jon a minute to remember what he was talking about. Vaughn rubbed the back of his head. "Vet saw you cruise by. She didn't know it was you, of course, until you pulled up later in the van." He adjusted his cap, resting his hand on the hood of his cruiser. "Chief called me in, too."

"We have the highest rate of domestic abuse in the Commonwealth, a thriving drug industry and he's worried about a dog—whose owner, by the way, violated the leash law and who was over the legal limit when he drove to the station?"

"It's not *just* the dog," Vaughn said, sharply. "It's not that goddamned simple."

Jon mumbled an apology, surprised at the other man's reaction. He had known Vaughn for almost twenty years and had assumed—erroneously, it seemed—that the man was impossible to ruffle. Vaughn shook his head and that flash of bitterness disappeared.

"It's the van," he said, sounding tired. "Principal reported it missing. Then the vet thing. That van might as well be a gift from God. This is grant money, kid. You lose something like DARE in a town like this, every politician within a thousand-mile radius of the State House will launch an anti-corruption task force to investigate."

"What did you tell him?"

This was Vaughn Whelan—the man who had single handedly kept Jon's record clean despite some serious errors in judgment on the young man's part. Vaughn shrugged.

Jon propped Matthew at an empty computer and found a website on Massachusetts marine life, then rapped on the chief's door, grinning.

Chief Skyles battled acid reflux, plantar fasciitis, asthma, as well as any number of seasonal conditions. When Jon pulled up the chair across from him, the bigger man sat forward, shoved his glasses into a crease on his forehead and folded his meaty hands together.

"What's going on with the van?" he asked.

"My car's a piece of crap, baby's a rotten sleeper, and Vicki needed some shut-eye."

"We'll get to you as the Family Man. First let's talk about police property, misused and noted." The chief stared at Jon who felt the first flicker of fear. Family Man?

"Maybe I misjudged how dearly the public values its DARE van, but this can blow over, right?"

"It could if a very angry vet hadn't called because you were not where you were supposed to be when you were supposed to be there. Even that we could have worked around. However, the next day when Parish went to get his dog's ashes—the vet had the poor animal cremated at no cost—he was told the thing might've lived if you had gotten there in time."

"The dog was bleeding out of its ear," Jon said, getting to his feet. "It was a goner, chief. Ask Vaughn."

The chief sighed as if he was a patient man, and Jon understood why Vaughn had looked exhausted. He had he told the chief what he knew *and* what he suspected.

"The point is, Sergeant, you didn't get him there. You were off, correct me if I'm wrong, visiting another esteemed town employee."

When Jon opened his mouth, the chief held up his hand. "And it isn't just Vaughn. You think you can keep secrets in a town where everyone's descended from the same fucked up tree trunk?"

Jon vowed to track Hedda Horn like a human satellite as soon as this blew over.

"Because you were on said visit, a bereaved pet owner believes we owe him $500—the going price of purebred pit bulls no matter how many kids they mutilate—and another few thousand for his pain and suffering. This last part, his attorney added."

Jon collapsed in his seat imagining the shit details he would be drawing, directing traffic around paving sites in August, re-routing cars past downed power lines during freezing rains in November.

The chief continued. "See, Sergeant, in this world you can go out, smoke dope, beat your kids, or steal a hundred bucks from the local convenience store and take out its Pakistani owner in the process, but if you really want to fire people up, let a goddamned dog die in a state-owned vehicle while you're out screwing around on your wife."

What imprinted on Jon's mind was an image he knew he would return to every sleepless moment the rest of his life: The white rise of Shar's throat when she reached for his dick, tossing her head back and laughing. The last moment he would feel such an empowering joy.

An hour later, Matthew perched in the swivel chair as his barber shaved his neck, leaving a tuft of white on the top of his head. Jon wondered how to do what he had been ordered to do as the barber tried engaging Matthew who responded with one-word answers. Jon felt the enormous effort it would be to carry on as if tomorrow would be the same as today. Few people, it turned out, ever pursued lawsuits against the police for something as small as what Jon had done. A guy like Clinton Parish wouldn't want to piss off the police. He needed time to cool off, the chief surmised, a reminder about how detectives establish hunches about certain citizens. However, in his immediate fervor, Parish had put a call in to the newspaper. The story would run.

"Call your girl," the chief instructed Jon. "Tell her she'll find herself alluded to in the papers. Hopefully, she has tenure or she'll lose her job by lunchtime. Then go home and save your marriage. Trust me. You'll spend your life groveling for every detail you can scrape together to pay off *any* ex-wife, but one who's the sympathetic party in a sordid newspaper story? You'll be delivering eggrolls in your spare time."

Jon called Shar from the pizza place while Matthew studied him from the table.

"Pretend you're out walking and we run into you," he said.

"This is even too kinky for me," she said, but she sounded scared and agreed.

In a town full of cockroaches and drug dealers, the beach was an anomaly, miles of sand lipped with white caps and dotted with rare sea birds. Jon had served citations to people over the years for clambering over dunes and disturbing nesting sites. His son escaped with a bucket while Jon sat on the top step of the boardwalk. No breeze lifted off the water. Grass grew past his shoulders but did not stir. Shar walked from the east as if she had been out strolling. He admired her resourcefulness. Adaptability, practicality, libido—these were wonderful traits in a mistress.

When she met up with Matthew, she knelt beside him as the boy lifted seaweed out of his bucket and placed it in her hand. She'll ask him to tell her everything he knows about his treasures, Jon thought, though he had never posed that question himself.

She left Matthew on the beach and plunked herself on a lower step, staring at the ocean.

"Hard to believe that, in a world this endless," she said, "you only get to live one life at a time."

The ride home was silent, but as they turned down his street, a stone fist lodging in Jon's stomach, Matthew said, "Why was Miss Dulcie crying?"

"She wasn't crying," Jon said. "She had sand in her eye. She had to hurry home to wash it out with water."

"The sand wasn't blowing." Matthew's voice was even but cold. "It was an unusually calm day."

———

Even with a bullhorn, it was impossible to hear Manfred Mancini over the approaching fire engines and the screams of the children. Smoke billowed from an open door in the cafetorium, a sickening chemical cloud that forced teachers to abandon the practiced drill routes and move children farther away from the building. They herded Batmans and green dragons, princesses, grim reapers and one bottle of ketchup onto the hill behind the playground, struggling to keep the children in countable lines. Once they had assembled their students in the far end of the parking lot, they held up green cards—all kids accounted for. Shar, in bell bottoms and a long black Cher-like wig, followed Stan Verran who wore a tracksuit and white sneakers, glued on sideburns. He pushed the boy in the wheelchair whose Ninja turtle mask sat atop his head. After last night's confrontation and the morning's newspaper, Jon would have expected Shar to call in sick, but maybe she had thought to face up to her role in a scandal, to get it over with. He was proud of her. She stopped, scanned her line and held up a red card. Child missing. Jon looked for Matthew's blonde head, his sleek, black wetsuit, checked again before he grabbed the megaphone from the principal and used it to announce to Mancini that Matthew was missing.

As Vicki arrived beside him, screaming Matthew's name, a firefighter emerged carrying a body. Through the smoke, the first thing

Jon could discern dangling over the firefighter's arms was the unmistakable shape of flippers.

—————

The school psychologist said Matthew had suffered some kind of emotional distress though the boy would not disclose what that was. He acted out as a way to bring attention to himself or that situation over which he had no control.

Vicki sat straight in her chair. In all the tumultuous weeks that followed her son's setting fire to the trash and placing it inside the custodian's closet to cause a chemical disruption, Vicki used a network of women to determine the best care possible for her little boy—doctors, therapists, school administrators—and told Jon that, as soon as she had taken care of her son, she would make a decision about their marriage.

"Until we get him what he needs, you stay put and pretend you are the most selfless human being on the planet. Because if you fuck up our son anymore than you already have, divorce will not be revenge enough."

He was desperate to please her, stunned at his attachment to his life.

He drove by Shar's house. Once Stan Verran's silver Mazda sat in the driveway, another time a green sedan Jon didn't recognize, its back seat loaded with boxes. She had tenure but resigned, put her cottage up for sale after parents complained that she was a terrible role model. Jon hated to imagine the parade of wife beaters and thieves, drug addicts and lap dancers who lined up outside Mancini's office eager to play the concerned parent. To whom could Jon bemoan the absurdity? To no one. Not now.

I'm one of them, he thought. I am and Vicki is and the children we have chosen to raise here.

He could predict how Shar would have responded to that, lying with him beneath several comforters, her socks on, her librarian's glasses and Chapstick on her bedside table. Down the street, the ocean would do what it does, its pattern a lulling rhythm: *What else? What else? What else?* Shar would have her hand on the light switch, hopeful she'd fall asleep before he drove away.

When you live all your life in one place, she would have said, you become a story anyone can tell.

ACKNOWLEDGMENTS

I am deeply grateful to the editors and slush pile readers of the following magazines in which my work has appeared: "No Sooner" in the *New England Review;* "All of a Sudden" in the *New England Review* and *The Drum;* "It Can't Be This Way Everywhere" on Huffpost 50; "Bewildered" in *Clackamas Review;* "On Loneliness and Other Theories" in *Slice;* "Having Your Italy" in *Oyez Review.*

Thanks also to Carolyn Kuebler and Stephen Donadio for their faith in me; to Brian Kologe, Miriam Novogrodsky, and Jane Donovan for getting it all started already; to Amy-Jo Conant, sweet magician, my first baby; to Rebecca Kinzie-Bastian for everything that has happened since those twin beds and that water bottle; to Sarah Yaw, my fellow goat, for wisdom, for all the pushes; to Brenda Boboige, who I have loved in several lives; to Noreen Cargill for so much more than room assignments; to Holly Robinson who, unbelievably, lives in my neighborhood (thank you, real-estate gods); to Lauren who has been there longest; to Teresa whose belief never wavers; to my sisters, Barbara Ann, Jeannie, and Patty, and my brother, Bill, for not calling me a freak even though they must have thought I was one; for my family—a wide, wide, wonderful circle—who make me feel part of something great and allow me to move from there; for my friends who want to know, who ask to listen; to my beautiful daughters Beatrice, Apphia, and Justina, for all those days we didn't go to the beach or to Canobie Lake because I was writing; to Dennis for this love of story and for this life that we share; to Pam Houston for her own stories and for choosing mine; to Bruce Wilcox, Mary Bellino, Sally Nichols, and the staff at the University of Massachusetts Press, and to the Association of Writers & Writing Programs; to my students who have given me a lifetime of discussing literature; and to readers.

Most of all to my mother who never believed that dreams are just dreams, and to my father: Dad, I am always listening for your voice.

CARLA PANCIERA is the author of two collections of poetry, *One of the Cimalores* and *No Day, No Dusk, No Love*. She has published fiction, memoir, and poetry in several journals, including the *New England Review*, *Nimrod*, *Chattahoochee Review*, and *Carolina Quarterly*. A high school English teacher, she lives with her husband and three daughters in Rowley, Massachusetts.